SEND FOR DR. MORELLE

Mrs. Lorrimer telephones Doctor Morelle claiming that she's in imminent mortal danger. In the morning her orange drink was poisoned, then she'd found a deadly snake in her bed and now toxic gas is emanating from the chimney and into the room! But is she really in danger? Is she mad — or perhaps feigning madness? Dutifully, Doctor Morelle sets off to the woman's house with Miss Frayle, his long-suffering assistant, who will soon begin to wish she'd stayed behind . . .

ERNEST DUDLEY

SEND FOR DR. MORELLE

Complete and Unabridged

LINFORD
Leicester

First published in Great Britain

First Linford Edition
published 2010

British Library CIP Data

Dudley, Ernest.
  Send for Dr. Morelle. - -
  (Linford mystery library)
  1. Morelle, Doctor (Fictitious character)
  - -Fiction. 2. Detective and mystery stories.
  3. Large type books.
  I. Title II. Series
  823.9′14–dc22

ISBN 978–1–44480–380–8

Published by
F. A. Thorpe (Publishing)
Anstey, Leicestershire

Set by Words & Graphics Ltd.
Anstey, Leicestershire
Printed and bound in Great Britain by
T. J. International Ltd., Padstow, Cornwall

This book is printed on acid-free paper

1

The Case of the Menaced
Mrs. Lorrimer

'Is that Doctor Morelle's residence?' The feminine voice sounded strained and distraught over the telephone.

'It is,' Miss Frayle assented. 'Who is speaking?'

'This — this is Mrs. Lorrimer, of Wimbledon. The Doctor knows me. Listen! I need his help urgently. Three — three attempts have been made to murder me today.'

'*What?*'

'I don't — don't know whether I will even be able to complete this telephone call.' The voice became shrill with hysteria. 'Even now I am in danger.'

'Hold on — I mean, just a minute. I'll call the Doctor.'

Doctor Morelle peered round his high-backed armchair where he was relaxing after a somewhat tiring day.

'It's Mrs. Lorrimer.' And, her tongue racing ahead of her anxious thoughts, Miss Frayle told him somewhat incoherently what the woman had said.

'Give me the telephone,' the Doctor commanded. Into the mouthpiece he snapped: 'What is the nature of your trouble. Mrs. Lorrimer?'

'Doctor! This morning my orange juice was poisoned. I took only a sip fortunately. Then — then when I went to lie on the bed a poisonous snake crept from under my pillow. I killed it with a shoetree. Doctor — are you listening?'

'Pray continue.'

'At this moment I am being stifled to death. It's poison gas! It's coming down the chimney. Someone — an enemy — is on the roof, sending the poison into this room.'

'What is the name of your assailant?'

'The — the name?'

'Yes — surely you must have some suspicion as to his identity.'

'It's — it's — ' The woman dwindled off in confusion, and then said suddenly:

'It's Hargreaves — Charles Hargreaves.' She gave an agonised moan. 'Doctor Morelle! You must come immediately.'

'Yes, yes, Mrs. Lorrimer,' he assured her — somewhat absently. 'Have any other attempts been made on your life today?'

'Several!' The woman paused, and then continued in a tornado of words. 'This morning I went to change my library book. A car deliberately swerved on the pavement and tried to knock me down — '

'And after that?' the Doctor prompted. His tone was almost somnolent.

'After that — then someone attempted to fracture my skull by throwing a window box from an upper storey window. It crashed right at my feet. Doctor — can you come immediately?'

'Yes, Mrs. Lorrimer. Pray remain indoors. On no account leave the room — stay near the telephone until I arrive.'

'Thank you! Oh thank you!'

There was a metallic click as the hook was depressed and the line disconnected. Doctor Morelle stifled a yawn of ennui.

'Oh, the poor woman!' burst out Miss

3

Frayle. 'To think that anyone should try to murder her. She's so lovely! What shall we do?'

'Proceed to Wimbledon,' the Doctor retorted with a heavy sigh. 'Circumstances permit of no other alternative.'

'Very well. I'll call a taxi.'

'Miss Frayle — ' the Doctor appeared to be making a decision. 'Wait!'

'Yes, Doctor?'

'First procure my emergency satchel, containing the hypodermic and narcotics,' he directed.

'Hypodermic?' she echoed, her eyes round with puzzlement.

'That is what I indicated.'

'But, Doctor, do you think Mrs. Lorrimer — ?'

'Pray do as I say before you induce in me the malady from which that person would appear to be suffering.'

With a sidelong glance at him, Miss Frayle hurried out of the study. Two minutes later, he was already sitting in a taxi outside his house in Harley Street, when she ran out with the equipment. He was now leisurely searching in a notebook for Mrs. Lorrimer's address. She had been a patient of his on a previous occasion. Although he took a long time to find it, he did not appear to be unduly flurried — in fact, he was obviously taking his time.

Miss Frayle tensed herself in suspense. Mrs. Lorrimer's life was threatened from all directions, and here was the Doctor actually dawdling! It was so unlike him.

Calmly he gave the taxi-driver the address.

Miss Frayle moved to the edge of the seat.

'And hurry up! It's a question of life and death — '

'On the contrary.' The Doctor countermanded her instruction. 'Proceed at your normal pace, driver,' and he added softly: 'This young lady, I fear, has a neurotic flair for the melodramatic.'

'Oh, Doctor, how can you?' she protested indignantly. 'Even if her life isn't threatened, she is obviously mad, and might do terrible things if we don't make haste.'

He blew out a cloud of cigarette smoke.

'You, too, recognised the symptoms of delusions of persecution, I gather?' he said with a supercilious smile.

'When you asked for the hypodermic, that gave me the clue. And my opinion is — '

'Your opinion would not only be useless, but it might also confuse the present issue. We are not even certain Mrs. Lorrimer is mentally deranged.'

'Then — then if she's not mad, she must be in danger,' pursued Miss Frayle.

He flung his cigarette through the open window.

'Is there not a third possibility?'

'You — you mean she might be pretending all this — deliberately.'

'Precisely.'

Miss Frayle's brow knitted in a puzzled frown.

'What makes you think that?' she queried.

'Mrs. Lorrimer, before she telephoned, had carefully evolved three separate delusions of persecution, namely, three different attempts on her own person — the poisoned orange juice, the snake in her bed, and the toxic gas emanating from the chimney. When I asked her if other attempts had been made, she rashly declared 'several', and then hesitated, while her prolific imagination conceived other methods by which murder could be committed.'

'And that hesitancy gave you the clue she was making it all up for some reason? That she really didn't have any delusions?'

'Precisely.'

'But why should she pretend she is mad?'

He studiously ignored her question, no doubt because it was unanswerable at this stage. Instead he said at a tangent:

'However we must not forget that even the simulation of madness is symptomatic of a neurotic, escapist temperament. Mental derangement does not always express itself in hard and fast manifestations. The symptoms can vary immensely.' He sat back in his seat and relaxed. 'I ordered you to procure the hypodermic as a precautionary measure. We may well arrive at Mrs. Lorrimer's residence, and discover her to be a raging lunatic — '

Miss Frayle's eyes became awed circles. 'Do you think she might be violent?'

'Quite probably. People possessed of delusions which take the form that they imagine people are trying to murder them, may become homicidal in what they imagine to be self-defence.'

'But this is terrible!' Miss Frayle exclaimed with a nervous squeak.

The Doctor permitted himself a sardonic smile.

'I have no fear but that I shall be able to cope with the situation with your invaluable assistance, my dear Miss Frayle.'

His quiet sarcasm escaped her.

'I wish I hadn't come now.'

'Your curiosity impelled you to do so. I did not request your presence.'

The taxi was traversing Putney Bridge. A grey, evening mist swirled from the Thames, and the sound of hooters from tugs seemed to add an eerie touch to the scene.

Miss Frayle shivered. 'I — I can't bear this — not — knowing,' she exclaimed. 'We don't know whether Mrs. Lorrimer is mad or not, and we don't know, if she isn't insane, why she's pretending to be.' She turned to the Doctor urgently. 'Will you be able to tell whether she's mad immediately?'

'Not necessarily,' he replied, lighting another Le Sphinx. 'Mentally deranged people often alternate between periods of cool rationality and raving mania.'

'You — you mean she might greet us normally and yet still be mad?'

'More than probable, my dear Miss Frayle,' he assented with irritating cool-ness. He wound up the window to shut out the cold night air. 'These morbid speculations are hardly constructive,' he commented in acid tones. 'To be more helpful, perhaps you can tell me if you ever witnessed Mrs. Lorrimer on the stage. She was an actress, was she not?'

'Yes — I saw her some years ago. She retired from the stage when she married Max Lorrimer.'

'Do you recollect what type of roles she portrayed?'

'Always something very dramatic. Rather over-dramatic, I thought; I remember all

London loved her. She really was a very beautiful woman — though, of course, you wouldn't notice that, Doctor! Oh, what a terrible tragedy for her — !'

The taxi had turned along a wide avenue, and the driver was peering out, to discover which side of the road the house would be situated. He put on the brakes. The house, set back from the road, along a short drive, was dark and squat, like some large jungle animal crouching, ready to spring.

Instead of a modern electric bell they discovered it was the old-fashioned bell-pull variety that clanged weirdly in another part of the house, a brief period of time elapsing before pulling the handle and the actual ringing of the bell.

The door opened and Doctor Morelle stepped inside, followed reluctantly by Miss Frayle.

'Doctor Morelle?' a mellow, respectful voice queried.

They turned to observe the butler who moved out of the shadows as he closed the door. He was a typical family retainer, tall and with erect carriage, kindly grey eyes and a well-shaven, pink face.

'The servants will be most relieved when I inform them that you have arrived,' he said pleasantly, and it was now obvious that behind his impassive manner was a hint of tense anxiety.

'Perhaps you will first inform Mrs. Lorrimer of my arrival,' the Doctor bade, ignoring the man's outstretched hands, which offered to take his hat, coat, and stick.

'Very good, Doctor. If you and the lady would be good enough to wait here — '

The butler moved swiftly, yet with perfect dignity, up the wide staircase.

'What a perfect pet!' Miss Frayle cooed, following him with her eyes. 'You don't see many servants like him nowadays. Why, he might have stepped out of a Victorian novel. I can just imagine him keeping the rest of the staff in order below stairs, and I think — '

She sighed as she realised that the Doctor was not listening to her. He was pacing across the hall, his lynx eyes darting from side to side. He walked across to a telephone, which stood on a small table. The L-Z directory was open at the M page. No doubt Mrs. Lorrimer had used this telephone to summon Doctor Morelle. Beside the directory was a thick volume entitled *The Encyclopaedia of Medical Knowledge*, and it was open at a chapter headed *Insanity*. One section, captioned *Paranoia*, was marked faintly in pencil. Carelessly thrown against a scribbling pad was a hand circular which bore the name Charles Hargreaves, Ltd.

Miss Frayle followed his contemplative gaze.

'Why, Doctor,' she gasped, 'this all fits together like a jigsaw — '

She broke off as the butler came down the stairs, his dignified carriage suggesting he was carrying an imaginary salver.

'Madam will see you,' he intoned, bowing stiffly from the waist. 'Pray follow me, please.'

He opened a door at the top of the stairs and announced them.

Miss Frayle stood close to Doctor Morelle as if for protection when they entered.

Mrs. Lorrimer was standing in the middle of the room watching the door. She walked across and grasped the Doctor's arm. Her hair was neatly coiffured, and she was soignée in her black hostess gown. Her features still contained that ethereal loveliness which had thrilled theatre-goers a few years ago. Though she was obviously distracted, she betrayed no patent symptoms of dementia.

'Doctor Morelle,' she began, in that melodious voice with its famous throaty timbre. 'Thank heavens you've arrived.' She glanced coldly at Miss Frayle. 'But you shouldn't have brought this young woman.'

'She is my assistant, Miss Frayle. I can assure you she will treat everything you may say with the greatest confidence.'

'Oh, I've no doubt about that!' Mrs. Lorrimer said quickly, and flashed Miss Frayle a synthetic smile. 'It's just that — that what I have to say is hardly suitable for the ears of — '

'But that's all right,' Miss Frayle put in quickly, determined not to be hustled out of what promised to be an interesting case. 'I might be able to help. The Doctor has always found my assistance most valuable in his cases.'

Doctor Morelle coughed, but refrained from comment.

Mrs. Lorrimer glanced across the room to a small recess over which was drawn a crimson velvet curtain.

'Well, don't say I haven't warned you,' she said with a little shudder. 'I am afraid what I have to tell you is a trifle — well, sordid.'

'Proceed.'

'First of all, I must confess that I had to use a trick to get you here. I had to make you think I was mad!'

'That I deduced,' Doctor Morelle said with a tinge of irritation. 'You had evidently studied the symptoms of paranoia from a medical book which is near the telephone downstairs. In addition you used the first name that your eyes alighted on in order to name the assailant. It was singularly careless of you to leave the evidence of your subterfuge so obviously disposed, Mrs. Lorrimer.'

'I — I was interrupted,' she explained, touching his arms coaxingly. 'Now, don't be cross with me, Doctor. I assure you I have not brought you here on a fool's errand. Something — something has happened since to make it all more terrible than I expected.'

The woman suddenly raised a finger to her lips.

'Just a moment — wait!'

Swiftly she walked across to the door, grasped the handle, turned it slowly and flung open the door. She peered outside and then closed it silently.

'What's wrong?' gasped Miss Frayle.

The other announced in a tense whisper: 'It's all right. I just wanted to make sure Craig, the butler, wasn't listening at the door. My husband's very jealous and sometimes I think he gets him to spy on me.'

The Doctor clicked his tongue impatiently. It appeared that there were far too many histrionics for his rational tastes.

'If you are not indisposed, why did you send for me?' he demanded sharply.

Mrs. Lorrimer looked at him with

tragic, limpid eyes.

'I was being blackmailed,' she said. 'He was coming again tonight for more money. I wanted you here to protect me — '

'Would it not have been more appropriate for you to have notified the police in the first instance?'

'I was afraid they'd say my husband would have to know,' she replied anxiously. Her perfectly shaped hands fluttered helplessly. 'You see, I'd written some letters to this man, and — '

'The police would have protected you by anonymity as they invariably do in blackmail cases. Really, Mrs. Lorrimer, you seem to be wasting my time.' He walked towards the door. 'You surely must be cognizant that I cannot expend my energy and genius on mere blackmail cases — '

'Yes, I realise that,' she said dully. 'That was why I had to trick you into coming here — why I had to pretend to be mad. I was desperate, you see.' She twisted her hands frenziedly. 'Don't go, Doctor. It's — it's no longer a mere case of blackmail now. It's much worse than that — '

'What do you mean?'

'It's — it's murder.' Again she clung to his arm. 'You must believe me. Just as I'd finished telephoning you, the man who has been blackmailing me staggered in through the front door. It wasn't locked. He'd been stabbed. I — I helped him upstairs, and he collapsed!'

'Good gracious!' Miss Frayle gasped.

Mrs. Lorrimer said: 'He must have arrived earlier than we'd arranged, and someone — out there in the drive — stabbed him.'

'Did he tell you the identity of the assailant?' said Doctor Morelle quickly.

'No, he — he couldn't speak. He — he died within a few minutes.'

'How horrible,' Miss Frayle gasped. 'Then if he died, his body is in this house — '

'In this room!' The woman's wide eyes became staring. She pointed a shaking hand across the room. 'He's over there, behind those curtains.'

'Ha . . . it is advisable that I examine the body.' Doctor Morelle traversed the room with long, raking strides.

'I drew the curtains across to — to hide him,' Mrs. Lorrimer said, with a shudder.

Doctor Morelle withdrew the curtains and on bended knees examined the body, which was in a huddled position. A yellow-handled carving knife was plunged into the man's back, up to the hilt.

'Hm ... yes, life is extinct,' he pronounced. 'He hardly makes an attractive corpse. Perhaps it would be advisable if I draw the curtains again.' He straightened himself and walked to the telephone, which was near the door. 'It is imperative that we summon the police.'

Mrs. Lorrimer ran across the room, and placed herself between the Doctor and the instrument.

'No, no, you mustn't!'

'It is essential, homicide has been committed.'

'But my husband — Think of his reputation — and mine, too. Neither of us can afford a scandal. I have another suggestion — '

Doctor Morelle appeared to be waiting with grim impatience for her to subside.

'I am a rich woman. I will give you anything — any money you wish. You will be able to use it for scientific research, for some good cause — '

He raised his eyebrows quizzically.

'And what, in return, am I expected to do?' he asked coldly.

'You — you must dispose of the corpse. You're a medical man. It should be easy for you. You can dismember it — use it for your experiments.'

Miss Frayle was attacked by a spasm of nausea at the cold-blooded effrontery of the woman.

'I warn you, Doctor,' Mrs. Lorrimer continued dramatically. 'If you use that telephone I'll kill myself.'

His impassive features betrayed no reaction either to the woman's monstrous suggestion or her suicidal threat. He stared at her silently, almost mesmerically, for fully thirty seconds. She drew back silently. Somehow, it seemed, she could not take her gaze from him.

In a slow, hypnotic voice, he intoned:

'You are overwrought, Mrs. Lorrimer. Soon you will be calm and relaxed. You

19

will face the future without apprehension. You are going to allow me to telephone the police, and you will not display any opposition . . . '

Deliberately he averted his gaze. Mrs. Lorrimer moved from the telephone. She seemed as though she was emerging from a trance.

'You were going to telephone, Doctor,' she murmured resignedly. 'I suppose it is the wiser course.'

'Assuredly.'

Miss Frayle had watched the extraordinary scene with ill-concealed fascination. It was truly amazing how such a *volte-face* in Mrs. Lorrimer's emotions could be accomplished by Doctor Morelle's uncanny powers of suggestion. He was now reaching for the telephone. At that moment the door opened. Miss Frayle spun round.

'Get away from that 'phone!' a voice barked.

Imperturbably Doctor Morelle continued dialling.

'He's got a gun, Doctor,' warned Miss Frayle, her eyes fixed on the squat middle-aged man in the doorway, who was determinedly pulling back the safety catch of a revolver.

'Max — be careful!' cried Mrs. Lorrimer.

Doctor Morelle calmly replaced the telephone, and regarded the intruder impassively.

'You are, I gather, Mrs. Lorrimer's husband?'

'I am,' the man replied. He set his jaw determinedly. 'This revolver, by the way, is fully loaded.' Lorrimer turned to his wife abruptly: 'Margaret, go to your room.'

She took a step forward, her arms outstretched pleadingly.

'Max, let me explain. They came to help me — they — '

'We'll discuss all that later,' the other retorted firmly. 'Now go to your room.'

Her shoulders shaking with convulsive sobs, Mrs. Lorrimer staggered through the doorway.

Immediately, the man slammed the door, and cocked his revolver menacingly.

'So you'd like to bring the police into this, eh?' he rasped.

Doctor Morelle walked calmly towards him.

'Another step, and I'll shoot.'

The Doctor shrugged his shoulders and halted.

'You are hardly behaving in an adult manner,' he said softly. 'I would diagnose you as being a case of retarded development.' He smiled thinly. 'Perhaps you do not realise that a man has been murdered. Your attitude will not help matters.'

Lorrimer made a great effort to control his voice.

'Forgive me if I don't seem cooperative,' he said. 'But when you leave here, which'll be in a moment, you'll be at liberty to do as you please.' He added menacingly: 'I just want to warn you against making fools of yourselves.'

'What do you mean?' Miss Frayle recovered her voice.

'Merely that if the police should call here they'll find nothing. No body — no murder! Understand? D'you think I'm going to let my wife get involved in this mess?'

'The police will take the Doctor's word

22

rather than yours,' challenged Miss Frayle, with unexpected spirit. 'You'll never get away with it.'

'No?'

'No!' echoed Doctor Morelle suddenly. In one second his body tensed and he leaped towards Lorrimer. Miss Frayle screamed above the revolver shot, and closed her eyes.

'I am unharmed, Miss Frayle,' the Doctor called out reassuringly.

She opened her eyes to see that Lorrimer was trying to break the Doctor's attempt at a ju-jitsu hold. The younger man had a definite advantage. Strenuously the Doctor was jerking at the wrist that held the revolver, Lorrimer's fingers were still on the trigger, as he tried to train the revolver on Doctor Morelle.

Realising the desperation of his position, Miss Frayle's eyes darted round the room urgently. A heavy ornate vase stood on the mantelpiece. She grasped it with both hands, and intrepidly moved towards the swaying figures.

'Hold on, Doctor! I'll hit him with this vase.'

She cracked down the vase wildly.

Next second Doctor Morelle collapsed, stunned.

'Oh! What have I done?' she gasped.

Max Lorrimer gave a grunt of satisfaction and ran a hand through his ruffled hair.

'Thank you, young woman!'

She rounded on him.

'It was your fault, you beast,' she flashed. 'You moved your head!'

'Very inconsiderate of me!' Lorrimer jerked the revolver to the door. 'You'd both better get out. I'll ring for Craig to help the Doctor. Perhaps this'll be a lesson to you to mind your own business.'

Miss Frayle was on her knees, lifting the prostrate Doctor's head.

'I think — I think I've killed him. Oh, this is terrible!' she moaned. 'Oh, Doctor Morelle!'

His eyelids fluttered open, and in her relief she let his head fall to the floor again.

At that moment the door opened, and the butler appeared. Despite the extraordinary scene that met his eyes he did not allow his dignity to be ruffled.

'You rang, sir?'

'Yes, Craig. The lady and gentleman are leaving, The latter will require your assistance.'

'Very good, sir,' murmured the butler as he moved towards the Doctor's outstretched figure.

'No nonsense from 'em. Get 'em out! Take this in case they need some persuasion. Here!'

'Yes, sir.' The butler took the gun as though it was all in the course of his normal duties.

'Well, hurry man. Come on!'

The butler coughed hesitantly. In a quiet firm voice he said: 'Don't you think we'd better wait until the police come, sir?'

'What the devil d'you mean?'

The other's respectful attitude changed. He held the revolver firmly trained on Lorrimer.

'Stay where you are, sir!' he ordered, 'or I'll shoot!'

'Why you — you must be mad, Craig,' Lorrimer blustered in blank amazement.

'Hand me that revolver.'

'I think not, sir.' He nodded reassuringly to Miss Frayle. 'Go ahead and 'phone Scotland Yard, miss.'

She hesitated — gaping with amazement.

'Pray telephone with all expediency, Miss Frayle!'

It was Doctor Morelle's voice, He was sitting up, rubbing his head painfully.

'Oh, yes, Doctor, yes.' She tried to steady her shaking fingers to dial the numbers.

Lorrimer was glowering at his butler malevolently.

'You'll regret this, Craig!' he threatened.

'It's *you* who's going to be sorry, sir,' Craig replied, still retaining a deferential tone. 'It's a terrible thing you have done — you or Mrs. Lorrimer — stabbing that poor man in the back like that.'

Miss Frayle was babbling excitedly into the mouthpiece.

'Hello, Scotland Yard ... ? I am speaking for Doctor Morelle. Is that Detective-Inspector Hood? We've caught

a murderer for you! Yes . . . the address
is . . . '

★   ★   ★

Two hours later, Miss Frayle carried a
cold water pack to soothe Doctor
Morelle's bruised head. She had been
fluttering round him maternally and not
even his terse sarcasms and reprimands
would check her ministrations. However,
his dark mood was evaporating now and
he was even puffing at a Le Sphinx with
some enjoyment.

'You know, Doctor, I couldn't believe
my ears when Inspector Hood arrived
and you told him to arrest the butler
Craig as the murderer,' she confided. 'He
was the murderer — yet he was the only
one who wanted to call the police.'

The Doctor exhaled a cloud of smoke.

'A transparent display of bluff,' he
replied. 'He had obviously been eaves-
dropping and realised that both Mr. and
Mrs. Lorimmer were behaving so suspiciously that the crime might well have
been attributed to either or both of them.

He evidently thought the safest course was to summon the police and divert suspicion from himself on to them. However, like nearly all murderers, he made one vital mistake — '

Dutifully Miss Frayle asked: 'What was that?'

'He said to Mr. Lorrimer: 'It's *you* who's going to be sorry sir, for what you've done. You or Mrs. Lorrimer — stabbing that poor man in the back like that!' Those were the exact words with which Craig, in effect, admitted his guilt. How did he know the man had been stabbed *in the back*? Mrs. Lorrimer never mentioned it so he could not possibly have overheard it.'

'And if he'd seen someone else commit the murder he would not have said, 'you or Mrs. Lorrimer'' deduced Miss Frayle brightly; 'he'd have known definitely.'

'Precisely! When he confessed at the police station, it appears Craig was working for the blackmailer, passing on information about Mrs. Lorrimer. Then when the man threatened *him* with blackmail, he killed him.'

She blinked through her spectacles at him with whole-hearted admiration.

'You're always so unerringly right, Doctor,' she said sincerely. 'You always seem to hit the nail on the head.'

'Hit? Head . . . ?' he repeated. He gazed at her in pained annoyance. 'Really, my dear Miss Frayle, I do not consider it exactly tactful of you to remind me that you — with violence and strength unbecoming to a young woman — actually struck a blow at — '

And, wishing she had bitten off her tongue rather than utter such tactless words, Miss Frayle braced herself to receive the full impact of Doctor Morelle's tirade of sarcastic recriminations.

2

The Case of the Bludgeoned Composer

On Sunday night at Church time, a twilight peace fell over West Park — that same indefinable quietude which dwells perpetually in a Cathedral city, though West Park was in fact a London suburb. Away from the main street, the trams and the Underground station, the roads widened and became tree-lined, and the four-storeyed Georgian houses bespoke the spaciousness of former generations. Fading glories, feudal traditions and pretensions still vaguely haunted Queen Anne's Terrace like a tired ghost. Just now the long straight road was deserted from end to end. Then a man in clerical grey cycled along, with dignified haste, on his high-handle-barred machine. A taxi cruised aimlessly, the very dilatoriness of the vehicle suggesting that the driver had lost all hope of picking up a fare. Towards the red pillar box a parlourmaid in uniform tripped undramatically, swinging her right hand, which held a picture post card. The dark windows of the houses stared like sightless eyes, until here and there, lights were put on, and curtains drawn like weary fallen eyelids. From round corners, quietly-behaved people appeared, walking with the leisured slowness of the English Sabbath. Folk were returning from church and the terrace now took on a certain restrained animation.

Only one woman walked on the right-hand side of the terrace. She looked straight ahead, her eyes focused on infinity as in her brain she still heard the church organ playing the recessional. She continued walking mechanically, enjoying negatively the abstract delight of a well-deserved leisure day and the comfort which the church service had brought her. Slowly her footsteps slackened, as upon her consciousness there impinged the sound of someone knocking at a door, The woman gazed round her in mystification. The knocking seemed to be coming from the door nearest to her. Yet strangely there was no one on the doorstep. She looked again as though she thought her vision was playing her tricks. The door was being knocked wildly — apparently by invisible hands.

Startled, the woman glanced round her. A few people were approaching in a faintly curious manner. The woman gazed in mild alarm at the door from which the knocking was coming. Her expression then lost some of its puzzlement as she realised that whoever was knocking at the door was knocking from the inside. Yes, that was it — apparently instead of knocking on the outside to be admitted, someone was knocking on the inside to be let out. However, on the principle that one should mind one's own business — especially on a Sunday — and that it is often impolitic to offer a helping hand until asked, the woman did nothing. Other people clustered about her, attracted by the sight of her gaping at a closed door. It was quite a minute before the group recruited a passer-by who had enough resourceful-ness to act in this emergency. A young man pushed up the steps and pressed his shoulder against the unyielding door at about the same moment as the knocking ceased.

'Hoy! Anyone there?' he shouted. There was no reply. He rattled the door knob and clattered the knocker. Then, bending down, he peered through a letter box. Shrugging his shoulders, the young man turned to the group.

'There's a light come on in the front room,' someone pointed out.

'Oh yes, look!'

A full score of eyes peered at the lighted window and at the figure of a woman who appeared in the front room of the house. The woman looked out of the window, and if she did see the people outside the house she was quite oblivious to them. She appeared to be inspecting the window. Then the amazed crowd observed her pick up a chair, move back from the window and, lifting the chair shoulder-high, she held it with the four legs before her as a buttress. The onlookers then saw her doing an astonishing thing. She took a running dive at the window. The pane crashed and splintered with the impact of the chair legs. Next second the woman, quite calmly, and still unmindful of her audience, was methodically picking out odd splinters from the window frame. When she had accomplished this to her obvious satisfaction, she surprisingly swung an agile leg over the window frame, and scrambled out, jumping on to the paving stones beneath her. She pushed through the crowd, and began to run in harrier manner down Queen Anne's Terrace, before anyone could summon the wit to ask her what was so obviously amiss. While the woman was still running down the terrace, Doctor Morelle and Miss Frayle were about to enter it from a side turning. The Doctor was returning from a lecture, and he was explaining to Miss Frayle how over-rated was the psychiatrist who delivered the lecture, and how futile were his seemingly erudite hypotheses.

He broke off as, out of the gloom, suddenly appeared the woman, now somewhat breathless, and, despite her general air of 'no nonsense' capability, rather distraught. She brushed against the Doctor, and after glancing up at him, evidently decided that he was more intelligent than the gaping morons who had silently watched her breaking out of the house. She halted.

'Telephone box?' she panted urgently. 'Where is it?'

Doctor Morelle regarded her calmly. 'I fear I am quite unable to satisfy your curiosity,' he murmured.

'You see, we're strangers round here,' Miss Frayle put in apologetically.

He rounded on her sharply.

'Miss Frayle, that was the exact cliché which I took great pains *not* to employ.'

'I mean I haven't noticed a telephone box.' Determined to be impervious to the Doctor's snubs, Miss Frayle turned to the woman sympathetically. 'I'm sorry. Is anything the matter?'

'Yes, but you can't help,' said the woman bluntly, almost rudely. She moved away, as though she was realising that she was wasting time by talking to strangers. Then, more to herself, she said: 'I must get a doctor at once.'

'A doctor?' queried Miss Frayle. 'Did you say 'Doctor'? Well, that's funny, because — '

'Coincidentally, and not comically, as my assistant would no doubt have you believe,' interrupted the Doctor pompously, 'I happen to be a physician.'

'D'you?' The question was almost insolent. Was the woman doubtful?

'I am Doctor Morelle.'

'Yes?' The woman remained unimpressed. 'Well, could you come quickly? It's Mr. Cornelius Jones — lives at Park House — about fifty yards away.' She spoke telegraphically, not wishing to waste words in what was obviously an emergency. 'He's been attacked — Hurry! He's unconscious.'

'I will come at once.' Already the Doctor was standing at her side, his gaunt figure leaning forward and his features looking even more saturnine in the evening gloom.

'Lucky I ran into you,' the woman shot over her shoulder as she raced ahead of them. 'I rent Mr. Jones's basement cheap because I do odd jobs for him. Score copying. He's a composer. Quite famous. Eccentric. Won't have the telephone. Nuisance.'

She continued in a breathless, clipped babble, keeping a few yards ahead of them.

'Extraordinary perfume!' Doctor Morelle observed softly to Miss Frayle. His finely chiselled nostrils quivered searchingly. 'Unusual that such an unfeminine creature should be so liberally adorned.'

'It is a little strong,' qualified Miss Frayle, refinedly restrained in her expression of opinion.

'Almost anaesthetically potent!'

The woman was glancing round impatiently.

'Can't you put a jerk into it, I say? I had to leave Mr. Jones alone while I came out to get help.'

'You say he had been attacked?'

'Yes, in the music room — over the head — while he was working.'

'Poor thing!' gasped Miss Frayle, blinking agitatedly through her spectacles.

'Bit of a shock to me,' the other went on. 'Went in just now with some supper for him — and there he was.' She halted opposite the house, where a few lookers-on still lingered. 'Here we are. 'Fraid you'll have to scramble through the window. Front door locked. Someone took the key. Don't know who. Probably Mr. Jones. Searched his pockets. Couldn't find it. Pretty grim.'

She paused on the top step and looked over the heads of the few bystanders as though they did not exist. She screwed her eyes in the gloom, as she listened to someone approaching, whistling.

'That's a policeman, I think,' the woman speculated. 'We ought to tell him, Doctor.'

'I think the person whistling is not in uniform,' the Doctor vouchsafed.

They stood on the steps, all peering into the darkness, and as they waited they heard the whistling growing nearer. It was a strange melody the man was whistling, not by any means one of the usual tunes that people whistle on streets, Now the approaching stranger began to hum it to the tonic-sol-fa.

'Sounds very like Mr. Wickham,' the

woman said quickly. 'Friend of Mr. Jones's,' she explained. 'He was expected this evening.' She cupped her hands round her mouth and shouted. 'That you, Mr. Wickham?'

The group heard the humming stop and the footsteps falter.

'Who's that?' came an elderly male voice from the gathering darkness.

'It's me,' called the woman ungrammatically. 'Me — you know Mary Denton.'

'Ah, is anything wrong, Miss Denton?' the pleasantly modulated voice inquired.

''Fraid so,' she nodded bluntly, 'Mr. Jones. Been knocked unconscious.'

'Dear me! This is regrettable. I was just going to call on him. I've been away — just got back — ' He joined them. Doctor Morelle could discern in the streetlamp illumination that he was a smallish built man, with pince-nez. 'I trust it's not serious. When did this happen?'

'Just now,' clipped Miss Denton. 'Been haring all over the show for a doctor. I've found one — '

'I am Doctor Morelle,' the Doctor introduced himself impressively hoping that he would get some respect from this new quarter. 'And this is my assistant, Miss Frayle. You are Mr. Wickham.'

'That's correct. Thank heavens you happened to be near. I do hope nothing untoward occurred to my old friend.' Then he added in a lower confiding tone, as though it would have been disloyal of him to speak the words loudly: 'Cornelius — I mean Mr. Jones — is a bit cranky and hates modern inventions like the telephone and so on. He had a bad scare some months ago when burglars broke in — and do you know — '

'Mr. Wickham!' Mary Denton admonished. 'The Doctor is anxious to attend Mr. Jones who is lying seriously injured.'

'Of course! Of course! How thoughtless of me — '

'Well come on, all of you. Window's open.' She was already athletically astride the frame, one leg in the room. 'It's easy if you lever yourself in!'

Doctor Morelle negotiated the window frame with creditable speed, though, despite Miss Denton's assurance, Wickham and Miss Frayle could make it only after a great deal of pulling and pushing and verbal encouragement. Inside the room the Doctor was saying:

'Was it really necessary to break this window?'

' 'Fraid so. Front door n.g. Back door locked up. Mr Jones had it done after the burglary,' she explained in her catalogue manner. 'Burglars broke in there. Downstairs windows all nailed up.'

'Have you any knowledge as to who would lock the front door and remove the key, and with what motive?'

'Haven't the foggiest.' She turned and glanced at Miss Frayle and Wickham who had at last negotiated the window.

'Everybody here? Come on. This way — Hurry!'

'This is dreadful — dreadful. Really deplorable!' Wickham was muttering ineffectually. 'My poor old friend — '

'There! There! It may not be as serious as we imagine,' Miss Frayle soothed.

Halfway along the hall Miss Denton was saying to Doctor Morelle in her most

41

disparaging manner: 'Hope you've had some experience of emergency cases, Doctor What's-your-name. I mean I hope you're not one of these hand-holding, pill-peddling doctors — '

'Miss Denton, may I inform you in all modesty,' he retorted grimly, 'that my elucidation of criminal cases, my surgical skill and my diagnostic ability are equalled only by your apparent ignorance and total lack of good manners.'

'Oh!' The imperturbable Miss Denton was not acutely abashed, however.

'What did you say your name was?'

'Doctor Morelle.'

'Sorry never heard of you. Not that I would. Never take any interest in anything but music. The Stravinsky school, of course. Jones is a genius, you know. Elemental.'

'Then perhaps you will understand this analogy,' the Doctor said icily, his heavy eyelids drooping with restrained menace. 'In the fields of medicine and psychiatry I am more advanced and universally respected than Mr. Jones is in his particular sphere of music.'

'So you're a genius, too,' she nodded briskly. 'Fine. World needs brains. We're going to get on together.'

'I fear not!' he replied, without regret.

The other shrugged rudely and pushed open a door, feeling along a wall for the light switch.

'He's in here,' she said quickly. 'Hope we're not too late.'

The Doctor's eyes narrowed as he glanced round the well-furnished room. On a long settee a heavily built man lay full length. An untouched supper tray lay on a sideboard. Doctor Morelle walked across to the settee and looked at the inert figure intently. Miss Denton joined him, while Miss Frayle and Wickham sought mutual commiseration near the door, as they gazed at the injured man.

'He was lying over the piano,' Miss Denton was stating. 'I moved him.'

'That must have required no little effort. He's a heavy man.'

'Yes.' Wickham edged two paces into the room, twitching his lips in anxiety for his old friend. 'Cornelius weighs nearly thirteen stones. Oh, poor, poor fellow.'

'Anyway, I managed to lift him,' Miss Denton said bluntly. 'I'm no weakling.'

'Apparently not,' murmured the Doctor. He stood upright, glared round him and fixed his eyes on his tremulous assistant. 'Miss Frayle, kindly refrain from behaving like a startled hen. Your assistance would at this time be appropriate. Pray tilt the table lamp this way.'

'Yes, oh, yes — ' She succeeded only in knocking the wrought iron lamp off the table. 'Oh dear, I can't — '

'Allow me, Miss Frayle — ' It was Wickham at her side, replacing the lamp carefully.

'Thank you,' the Doctor acknowledged. He turned his back on Miss Frayle, speaking over his shoulder: 'Please be seated, Miss Frayle, before with your clumsiness you demolish any more of Mr. Jones's priceless antiques. If you cannot be helpful kindly be non-obstructive.'

'Oh, all right, Doctor.' She sank into an armchair, feeling rather like a schoolgirl who has been reprimanded and told to sit in a corner.

Silently, with every person in the group

watching him, Doctor Morelle continued his examination. 'Hm. No fracture of the skull,' he pronounced, after an interval. 'Pulse weak, respiration — slow — ' He straightened himself and regarded Miss Denton distastefully.

'Have you any idea when this occurred?'

'Couldn't have been more than half an hour ago. I heard him playing then.'

'Did you not hear sounds of a struggle or a cry for assistance?'

'Can't say I did. I was playing records on my gramophone in the basement.'

'Yet you heard the pianoforte above your gramophone instrument?'

'No — I heard him when I changed a record.'

'I see!' He nodded thoughtfully. 'Is there anyone else in the house other than ourselves?'

'No — no one at all.' She ruffled a strong, conical-fingered hand through her short wiry hair. 'I say, is he — will he live? Terrible loss to music if he doesn't. Mr. Jones — genius. Irreplaceable, y'know.'

Doctor Morelle did not answer her. Miss Denton approached nearer and his nostrils quivered allergically. 'Miss Denton, would you have the goodness to make some tea — rather weak?' he requested.

'Oh, very well,' she said ungraciously, and stumped out of the room.

The Doctor then blew his nose vigorously. 'That perfume was quite stifling,' he commented. He regarded Wickham questioningly. 'Does the young woman usually wear such overpowering perfume?'

'I can't say that I've noticed it,' Wickham said, and he ventured nearer to the couch. 'Dear me, I'm terribly anxious, Doctor. How is he?'

'A clear case of concussion sustained as a result of a blow on the top of the skull. Appreciable swelling — '

'He'll be all right, won't he?' urged Wickham, nervously polishing his pince-nez and rubbing his eyes before replacing the lenses. 'I'm really most upset — '

'Pray calm yourself,' the Doctor directed imperturbably. 'I have no doubt that Mr. Jones will recover.'

'Good! Good! Ah, look — '

All eyes were turned on the injured

composer, as they heard him give an agonised groan. His lips twitched slightly, and there was a flickering of his eyelids.

'He's opening his eyes,' exclaimed Miss Frayle, jumping up and upsetting a Louis Quinze card-table. 'Oh, I'm sorry, Doctor, I don't know how it happened,' she flustered. 'I just touched it — '

'Silence, Miss Frayle. Mr. Jones is attempting to speak, no doubt to identify his assailant.'

The composer's lips were moving. He seemed to be mouthing the words but could not summon the breath to speak to them. He made an effort to raise his head from the cushion but sank down again. Doctor Morelle knelt by the settee, and placed an ear close to the man's lips.

'Oh, my head!' the man groaned. 'Did I faint or what happened? I — I was at the piano.' The man's brow creased in strained bewilderment. Then his brow cleared slightly. 'Yes, I remember now. I'd just worked out that theme for the third movement of the sonata . . . ' Cornelius Jones made an effort to focus his gaze, and looked past the Doctor's shoulder at

Wickham, who was gazing down at his friend with ineffectual commiseration. Jones smiled at him in recognition.

'I want you to hear it, Wickham. Help — help me to the piano and I'll play it.'

'Yes, yes, but you mustn't talk now,' Wickham murmured soothingly.

Doctor Morelle noticed the pupils of the injured man's eyes contracting to pinpoints. He spoke close to his ear. 'Were you attacked, and by whom?'

'Attacked!' The other gazed at him blankly. 'Don't know.'

His eyelids closed. He sighed heavily, and the Doctor managed to catch the whispered words:

'Didn't see — anyone.'

'He's lost consciousness again,' Miss Frayle pointed out unnecessarily.

'Your flair for stating the obvious becomes increasingly apparent,' the Doctor observed in acid tones. He flicked a flame against the lip of his Egyptian Le Sphinx, and snapping the cap of his lighter into place, addressed Wickham through a cloud of smoke. 'Would you be good enough to find a call-box and telephone Harbeck

Two Thousand? It's a nursing home.'

'Harbeck Two Thousand,' repeated Wickham slowly. 'Yes. Doctor. What shall I say?'

'Merely acquaint them of the facts and have them dispatch an ambulance to this address without delay.'

'Yes — yes, I'll do that. Only too glad to help Cornelius.' He shook his head gravely at the prostrate man. 'Poor fellow — '

'And hurry.'

'Yes — yes.' Muttering to himself, he hurried to the door.

Miss Frayle leaned forward on her chair. In a soft, apologetic voice she ventured: 'Doctor — ?'

'Yes?'

'May I ask you something?'

'If it will contribute to the elucidation of this mystery, you may,' he conceded magnanimously.

'What exactly did Mr. Jones say when he recovered consciousness? I couldn't quite catch it all.'

'Ah!' His exclamation was almost explosive. 'So your inquiry is merely prompted by curiosity.'

'Not entirely; you see I have a theory, Doctor.' She blinked at him questioningly. 'Did Mr. Jones name his assailant?'

'He did not.'

'Or did he say anything about perfume?'

'No.'

Miss Frayle's hands fluttered hopelessly. 'Then I'm afraid that knocks my theory on the head.' She looked fearfully at Mr. Jones's injured head. 'Oh, why did I say that?'

The Doctor bowed mockingly. 'Thank you for your valuable contribution,' he said with thinly-veiled sarcasm. 'Perhaps there are some other points on which you would care to be enlightened while I am apparently being submitted to cross-examination.'

'Very well — who do you think would do such a devilish thing?'

'I doubt if the authorities will attribute it to a denizen of the nether regions!' he retorted enigmatically. 'Though robbery would doubtless be the motive despite the fact that nothing seems to have been taken. It would appear by the pictures, antiques and various ornaments with which he has surrounded himself, that Cornelius Jones is a successful musician.'

'If you ask me, although I know you wouldn't dream of doing so,' Miss Frayle said, 'I think the guilty person is — ' She suddenly broke off, her eyes widening like saucers as she perceived a figure bearing a tea tray entering the room. 'Why, Miss Denton!' She gave a nervous laugh. 'Haven't you been quick?'

'On the contrary,' the Doctor contradicted, 'Miss Denton has been an exceptionally long time.'

'Couldn't find the milk,' grunted the woman. 'Well, here it is.' She banged the tray on the table.

'Splendid!' The Doctor rubbed his hands together. 'Miss Frayle will pour it for me. She knows precisely how I like it.'

'You — ?' Miss Denton glared. 'I thought it was for Mr. Jones. Well, I think that's a bit thick! Having me haring about, because you want a cup of tea!'

'Precisely,' he said with cold menace, 'and you would oblige me if you would repair to Mr. Jones's bedroom and pack a suitcase so that he may be removed to the nursing home in comfort.'

'Nursing home? Suitcase? Don't understand.'

'I speak clearly, do I not? Come now. At once, please. Hurry!'

'Oh, very well.'

She stamped noisily out of the room, after giving him a malevolent glare.

'Really, I find that woman to be even more exasperating than you, Miss Frayle!' he commented.

'She looked as though she could kill you!' Miss Frayle declared as she arranged the tea things. 'Now what I was going to tell you before she came in was — '

'Silence. He appears to be recovering consciousness again.'

They looked closely at the injured man, who stirred dazedly.

He groaned and faintly his voice called: 'Wickham . . . Where are you?'

Through half-closed eyes he stared at Doctor Morelle.

'Ah, there you are, Wickham, dear fellow . . . ' he whispered.

'He's delirious,' Miss Frayle breathed. 'He thinks you're — '

'Bring the music — the music!' Jones said confusedly. 'I want to show you — show you the new theme — you're the first to hear it . . . '

Doctor Morelle signalled urgently to Miss Frayle, who passed him a sheet of manuscript foolscap from its ledge on the piano.

'Here's the music,' said the Doctor, bending over the injured man.

'That's a good chap,' whispered Mr. Jones. 'If — if you'd read out the notes — the last few bars I've written down. Yes, where your finger is — read them out.'

'It's in the key of C.'

'Yes, yes.'

Doctor Morelle hummed the notes softly and slowly: 'G — C — E — F — G — B flat — A — E — G — F — '

Miss Frayle, listening, felt vaguely she had heard the tune before and dismissed the composer as not such a genius as Miss Denton had described him, if he had to borrow from other musicians!

Jones groaned and closed his eyes.

'Lost consciousness again,' murmured the Doctor, and an enigmatic expression had appeared in his eyes. He bent over the inert figure. 'Hm. Pulse no worse — respiration rate about the same.' He moved to a table to stub out a cigarette. 'Mm. Wickham's a long time telephoning for that ambulance.'

'It would probably take him half an hour to get through that window,' Miss Frayle pointed out, 'and another half hour to find a telephone box — another half hour to remember the number, and another — '

'Please, Miss Frayle! I find your tautology a trifle exhausting.'

'Well, here's your tea, Doctor,' she passed him the cup and saucer. He sipped it, then walked across to the piano and began to reconstruct the crime.

'He was evidently sitting here, playing the piano and marking the score — yes, the pencil is here. Someone evidently entered that door silently, traversed this thick carpet, approached from behind and administered him a heavy blow over the head.'

'I can't believe anyone would do such an awful thing!' Miss Frayle exclaimed, 'Except — '

'While I, for my part, cannot imagine him knocking himself insensible! A little more tea.'

She almost spilled the tea as Miss Denton appeared bearing a suitcase.

'Here it is. I've just thrown everything in.' She looked at the injured man. 'Have you done everything you can for him before the ambulance arrives?'

The Doctor reassured her with icy patience.

Miss Denton then shut the door with unnecessary noise. She faced the Doctor defiantly, her hands planted firmly on her hips.

At that moment the light went out, leaving them in complete darkness. Miss Frayle uttered a stifled scream and fell headlong over a chair.

'Someone's switched them out!' she shrilled. She felt somebody brush past her as she lay prostrate. 'Help me!' She struggled up, knocking her head against the piano. 'I'm being attacked!'

'If an attack on you would silence you, Miss Frayle,' came the Doctor's terse voice from the darkness, 'it would indeed be refreshingly fortuitous.'

She saw the flame of his lighter, and could make out his saturnine profile as he walked to the light switch and clicked it up and down;

'Apparently the illumination was not extinguished from here.'

'Burnt out fuse!' Miss Denton was saying. 'Often happens.'

'Then it had better be attended to without delay. Kindly lead the way to it.'

He held open the door, and Miss Denton strode ahead of him.

'Don't leave me here, Doctor,' urged Miss Frayle tremulously, skirting pieces of furniture.

'Hurry then!'

'It's near the larder,' Miss Denton directed.

Out in the hall the Doctor laid a restraining hand on the woman's arm. Then he deliberately snapped down the cap of his lighter, leaving them in total darkness again. He heard men's voices arguing in a front room. He moved forward, listening.

'I tell you it's a mistake,' a man was saying. 'You're wasting your time and mine.' His tones were cultured.

'Ho am I? We'll see about that!' a gruffer voice was saying. 'Nar then, me lad, don't you be trying any of your monkey tricks — '

Miss Frayle caught on to the edge of the Doctor's jacket.

'I can hear voices,' she fluttered.

'Since the voices were of full volume they would be certain to impinge even on the most unreceptive ears,' he snapped. 'Kindly release your hold on my coat.'

'Oh, it's terrible being in the dark, not able to see anything — '

She broke off as the door of the front room was opened, and a shaft of light from a heavy torch shone in their faces.

'Who's there?' called Miss Denton.

'It's P.C. Allen,' the gruff voice called. 'Sorry to startle you. Just caught a man getting out of your front window. He gave me a bit of a struggle, but I've got him all right.'

Miss Frayle kept well behind the

Doctor for protection. He stepped forward in front of Miss Denton.

'Excellent officer,' he observed. 'Unfortunately the illumination is not operating. Will you accompany us to the basement, together with your prisoner?'

'Right-o, sir.'

'Now, Miss Denton, kindly lead the way.'

Miss Denton became strangely taciturn as she took them to the basement. The Doctor examined the fuse-box and then pressed down a rod, which controlled a double switch. Immediately the lights came on.

'Apparently someone deliberately extinguished the lights by the master switch. Now, let us examine your prisoner, officer.'

He regarded a sullen, well-dressed, clean-cut man of about thirty, who was being held by the massive policeman. The man glared at the Doctor with silent defiance.

'Refuses to give his name, sir,' the policeman grunted.

'You intercepted him climbing out of the window into the street, I take it?'

'S'right, sir.'

'What were you doing here?' snapped the Doctor to the man.

'Nothing — I mean — dash it all . . . I was just going home and — ' the man broke off incoherently. He turned his gaze to Miss Denton almost pleadingly. 'You tell them, Mary.'

She pushed into the group and faced the Doctor.

'He was here at my invitation,' she explained. 'Quite simple. I invited him for tea. We were listening to my records, didn't want any scandal. His job, y'see.'

The Doctor rounded on her angrily.

'Did you not inform me that there was no person in this house other than ourselves?'

'Yes.'

'Then you were guilty of a deliberate fabrication.'

'I s'pose so. Didn't see why Ronnie should be brought into it.' She pouted brazenly. 'We're old friends. Platonic. Same tastes in music. Mr. Jones wouldn't let me have visitors in the house. Stuffy. Had to sneak him in.'

'Yes, that's perfectly true,' the young man insisted. 'Mary's no more to blame than I am.'

'Perhaps having been discovered in one falsehood, Miss Denton, you would now oblige us by telling the whole truth,' the Doctor suggested icily, 'unless, of course, both of you would prefer to be detained in custody.'

'Oh, all right. But I don't think I've told any more lies. It was I who suggested to Ronnie to put out the lights. But I wanted to make sure that the first-aid on Mr. Jones wouldn't be hindered by the lights being put off. I fixed a signal. When I came up with the suitcase, I banged the door noisily. That was a signal for Ronnie to put out the lights and get away. Thought he stood a better chance of getting out in the dark, y'see.' Her defiant manner suggested that she considered she had done nothing underhand. 'Satisfied, Doctor?'

Doctor Morelle made no reply.

'Mary's speaking the truth,' the young man declared, more calmly now. 'Honestly I don't know anything about the attack on Mr. Jones. If I'd been able to help, I'd have told you I was here.'

P.C. Allen pulled at his moustache. 'What's all this here about?' he demanded. 'What's been happening, Doctor?'

'Attempted robbery with violence. Perhaps even attempted homicide.'

'Cor!' The policeman gripped the young man tightly. 'I'd better handcuff this bird.'

'That won't be necessary,' the Doctor declared. 'I do not consider he will be foolish enough to attempt an escape. Moreover, he is innocent.'

'Ho, he is, is he? Well, who did it then? Tell me that.'

'All in good time,' the Doctor retorted, nonchalantly lighting a Le Sphinx. He began to walk up the basement steps, calling over his shoulder. 'I think, officer, it might be timely if you would assist me to break open the front door, so that the injured man may be conveyed by stretcher to the ambulance. And also,' he continued laconically, 'so that the guilty person will not have the inconvenience of gaining entrance via the window.'

'You mean you expect the guilty party to come back?' P.C. Allen gaped.

'Precisely! Unless my knowledge of psychology is at fault — '

A few minutes later, the front door was forced and stood wide open. The group clustered tensely round the open door.

They did not have to wait long. There was the clang of an ambulance bell growing nearer, now traversing Queen Anne's Terrace. It drew up outside Park House. Two white-coated attendants jumped out with a stretcher, followed by Wickham who puffed up the steps. Miss Frayle ran down to assist him.

'Dear me, I had such a time, getting through to the nursing home,' Wickham flustered. He smiled at the Doctor. 'Hope I haven't been too long — '

'No — no. You have been of great assistance.' A supercilious smile touched the corners of Doctor Morelle's lips.

'Don't worry now, Mr. Wickham,' Miss Frayle insisted sympathetically.

The Doctor wheeled on his heels and fixed the policeman with a glare.

'This gentleman, for whom my assistant is showing such solicitude, bears the name of Wickham,' he said in a voice smooth as silk. 'He is a dangerous man. He committed an unprovoked and brutal attack upon Cornelius Jones.'

Miss Frayle released her hold on Wickham and sank to the floor in a half-faint. Unchivalrously, Wickham made no attempt to catch her as she fell.

★   ★   ★

Later, in the Doctor's study, Miss Frayle, somewhat pale and not at all her usual self, observed weakly:

'Mr. Wickham seemed such a harmless man. It just shows you can't always tell — '

'Precisely, Miss Frayle,' he murmured with quiet satisfaction. 'As you so eruditely reflect, appearances are often deceptive.'

'I felt sure Miss Denton had done it. She was so unfeeling — so aggressive.'

'Yes, distinctly unpleasant. Oddly uninhibited, however,' he speculated, enjoying his Le Sphinx, 'which prompts one to wonder whether inhibitions have a mellowing effect on temperament. Interesting.'

'I think you were wonderful, Doctor,'

she put in with open-mouthed admiration.

'I am constrained to agree with you,' he nodded. 'Modest as I am, my dear Miss Frayle, I must say my prognosis in that case was brilliant, quite brilliant.'

'I'm glad you're pleased.' She then framed her inevitable question with dutiful incredulity. 'However did you know Mr. Wickham was guilty?'

He leaned back in his chair and exhaled a cloud of cigarette smoke ceilingwards.

'Although the attack upon Cornelius Jones might seem to have been made by some unknown burglar,' he said, 'it quickly became apparent to me who had committed the crime — namely Wickham. The clue pointing to him, and upon which I seized was the musical theme the composer had completed at the moment he was struck down.' He paused impressively.

'Go on, Doctor.'

'Wickham, when we met him outside the house, said he was about to call on Jones, intimating he had not seen him before that night. Yet the tune he was whistling when he first saw us was the very theme the composer had written only a short while ago that evening. Wickham could not have known those particular bars of music unless he had heard the composer playing them on the piano as he wrote them down.'

'Forgive me interrupting you, but — '

'What is it, Miss Frayle?'

'When you read his music to Mr. Jones did you at once recognise the notes as being those Mr. Wickham had whistled earlier?' she asked wonderingly.

'Certainly.'

'That was awfully clever of you.'

'I'm glad you're pleased!' the Doctor commented icily. 'It was relatively simple . . . Remember the notes?' He sang softly in tempo. Miss Frayle recalled ruefully how she had thought the composer had borrowed the tune from some other musician.

'But why did he do it, and how did he get into the house?'

'He was in desperate financial straits. Miss Denton, as she later admitted, left the front door open so that her — er — platonic friend could call on her, without having to resort to ringing the bell, which might have given Jones grounds to suspect that she was receiving a clandestine caller. After the young man had entered, he apparently left the front door ajar. Wickham entered a little later, proceeded to the music room, attacked Jones with intent to rob him. But, fearful he had killed him and panic-stricken with remorse, he had rushed away without taking any of the valuables for which he had come.'

'Why was the front door locked and the key removed?' Miss Frayle pursued.

'The key was later found in Wickham's pocket. He had deliberately re-locked the door and removed the key so that help would be delayed in coming to Jones. He hoped that Jones would succumb to his injuries meanwhile, fearing that the man, if he lived, might be able to identify his assailant.'

'It all works out as completely as a jig-saw.'

The Doctor stubbed out his cigarette

and paced the length of the room.

'If you have recovered from your faintness, and no longer feel tired, my dear Miss Frayle, I feel it might not be inappropriate to make some notes while this case is fresh in our memories,' he said.

'You mean notes for your memoirs, Doctor?'

'Precisely!'

She looked at him anxiously through her spectacles.

'It won't be necessary to state that — I — that I fainted so foolishly, will it?' she queried embarrassedly. 'No one will be interested in that.'

'On the contrary, I feel the incident makes a telling denouement, and provides a graphic delineation of your gullible character.'

She started indignantly. 'I don't agree with you at all, Doctor — '

'Whether you agree or disagree concerns me not in the slightest,' he murmured abstractedly. He gestured irritably to his notebook. 'If you would merely be good enough to take down as I dictate?'

'Yes, Doctor.'

'Thank you! And in future — '

She knew what he was going to say — and in self-defence she said it for him in a mock querulous tone: 'And in future will I remember I'm employed in the capacity of assistant, and as such am required not to voice my opinions one way or another unless asked — which will be never.'

He smiled at her thinly. 'You have taken the words out of my mouth, my dear Miss Frayle!'

'I thought I'd save you the trouble.'

'Um — yes,' he observed dubiously. 'Well, I was about to commence dictating. Yes, an intriguing affair — singularly heavy perfume the woman wore. However to proceed.'

'I'm quite ready, Doctor.'

'Then we must not over-tax your patience, Miss Frayle,' he said with smooth menace. He began dictating: 'The circumstances under which I first met Cornelius Jones, the composer, were unusual, not to say, dramatic. It was one spring evening, when Miss Frayle and myself were returning from a lecture given by a somewhat over-rated psychiatrist. We were traversing the rather deserted neighbourhood of West Park, and as we turned a corner into Queen Anne's Terrace, out of the gloom suddenly appeared a woman, breathless and somewhat distraught. My assistant, Miss Frayle — '

Miss Frayle sighed as her pencil coursed over her notebook. Life, she thought, was recurrently like attending a cinema performance. Continually she was prompted to think: 'This is where I came in . . . '

3

The Case of the Haunted Holiday

Miss Frayle was constrained to believe Doctor Morelle had taken leave of his acutely-developed senses when, one morning noiselessly entering the study she found him putting his tongue out at himself in the mirror.

Seeing her fleeting reflection, he snapped tersely over his shoulder:

'Procure your pencil and prepare to inscribe some notes.'

Quite oblivious of her open-mouthed amazement, he contorted his lean face and again protruded his tongue in the mirror. Miss Frayle watched him with growing trepidation. The heavy strain of recent work had undoubtedly unbalanced his mind, she decided. Brilliant people were often on the borderline. She sat on the edge of her chair, ready to rush to the door should he become violent.

Goggling through her spectacles, she now saw him standing close to the mirror with his eyes screwed up tightly, as though he was trying to shut out some horrible hallucination. Suddenly he opened them and glared at himself with what she could only describe as a menacing expression. He then strode to the window and looked fixedly for a few seconds at the naked sunlight that poured into the room. Returning to the mirror, he again stared mesmerically at his own reflection. He swung round and uttered one terse word at her with such suddenness her spectacles almost fell from the tip of her nose.

'Commence!'

'Commence what, Doctor?' she stammered nervously.

'Inscribing from my dictation, of course,' he snapped, and added: 'Really your behaviour is most abnormal this morning. Now commence your hieroglyphics.' He dictated: 'Symptoms: inertia and — er — irritability — ' He paused. 'Would you say irritability, Miss Frayle?'

'I — I daresay,' she murmured, deciding it might be the safer course to humour him.

'Lingual membrane discoloured,' he continued his dictation smoothly, 'symptomatic of liver disorder. A slight condition of tachycardia — ' She did not know how to spell the word, but in his apparent state of dementia she dared not ask him. 'Have you got that, Miss Frayle?'

'Y — yes, Doctor.'

'Tachycardia symptomatic of nerve strain and over-smoking. Abnormal reaction of the optical pupils to illumination. Prognosis — positive. Treatment — a few days' complete relaxation in quietude and change of air.'

A glimmering of understanding shone in Miss Frayle's face.

'Who's this diagnosis for?'

'For myself, of course! Who else?'

She gave a little laugh of relief. 'You had me quite alarmed. For a moment I thought — thought you were delirious!'

'I presume it behoves me to explain,' he said, and looked at her with sardonic compassion for her limited intelligence. 'I fear, Miss Frayle, I am apt to overestimate your obviously very undeveloped powers of deduction. It ought to have been patent to the most moronic mind that I was conducting a medical examination upon myself, and not, as you apparently chose to believe, indulging in an attack of compulsion neurosis.'

She straightened her spectacles: 'I'm sorry, Doctor.'

Mechanically he reached for a cigarette from the skull container.

'Did you say, tachycardia?' she queried mischievously. 'Symptomatic of overindulgence in nicotine?'

Undeterred, he applied the flame of his lighter to the Le Sphinx, and regarded the tip of the cigarette attentively.

'You may delete that from your notes,' he said briskly. 'Now, as we are both to indulge in a quiet vacation, I think it obligatory on both of us to preserve harmonious relations.'

'You mean we're going on a holiday!' she said brightly, thrilled at the prospect of a change of air and scene.

'Precisely!'

She snapped her notebook shut and pushed it in a drawer. She stretched out her arms as though to symbolise the prospect of freedom.

'A holiday!' she breathed, 'that will be lovely.'

'Indeed, I trust so,' he commented with a slight hint of warmth in his voice.

'Where are we going?' Her eyes were wide with anticipation.

'To Sevenmeads,' he replied, 'a rather attractive though slightly pseudo village near the Thames Estuary. Fortuitously I received an invitation in the matutinal post from my old friend, one Ronald Hopbridge, who has a commodious and well-run residence on the outskirts of Sevenmeads. He asks me to stay for the weekend. You, too, are invited.'

'Oh, how kind of Mr. Hopbridge!'

'I prognosticate we shall discover him to be the host par excellence. He will respect the necessity for the quietude of his guests, not demanding and not giving too much of tedious conversational badinage. You may now commence to pack my impedimenta, and determine that everything is in order preparatory to our departure.'

'I'll see everything's ship-shape before we go.'

'No doubt for once I will be able to rely on your efficiency, since this is obviously a duty which you relish.'

'You can rely on me, Doctor,' she replied briskly; she went quickly out of the room.

In the early afternoon they were ready to start, and she was glad to see that despite his reluctance to show enthusiasm he was, nevertheless, evincing a certain amount of cheerfulness as he steered the car over Putney Bridge, and actually whistling to himself.

'When we arrive at Sevenmeads,' he said, as he unwound the window to admit fresh air, 'you will kindly oblige me by not mentioning to our host that I have been at all unwell. I wish to forget my physical condition as far as possible.'

'I see,' she nodded, and glanced at the open window. 'Don't you think you ought to close the window? You might catch cold in your rundown state.'

He clicked his tongue impatiently and snapped:

'That is precisely the type of remark I did not wish you to make. I refuse to be the victim of your repressed maternal instincts.'

'I was only trying to be sympathetic,' she pouted.

'No doubt, however, sympathy is a dangerous reaction which, among the mentally unstable majority is prone to produce a feeling of self-pity — a most vulgar emotion.'

The rest of the journey was endured in silence, apart from the Doctor's spasmodic whistling, and as his repertoire consisted solely of the more subtle excerpts from Bach's Cantatas, Miss Frayle was unable to appreciate it.

A sharp shower had cleared the sultry air, and the cobblestones of Sevenmeads shone in the sunshine. The Doctor waved his right hand airily as they drove down the main street.

'You will observe, Miss Frayle, with, I hope, a feeling of nausea, civilisation's ill-placed concessions to past decades,' he commented scathingly. 'Remark the petroleum pumps disguised as beehives; the faked old timber of the residences and the modern establishments of comestibles where misguided people strive to attain an impression of antiquity.'

'There are a lot of 'Ye Olde Tea Shoppes', aren't there? Just look at that place — 'The Pixie Market — home-made cakes and morning coffee',' and she added a flash of repartee which she thought he would especially appreciate. 'Arts and crafts, plaster masks, woollen dolls and leatherwork as a sideline!'

'To sneer at that which others take seriously is, I feel, somewhat uncalled for,' he commented coldly.

She bit back the obvious retort that this was almost his invariable habit. For the sake of peace she merely murmured in agreement.

They approached the Hopbridge residence, and left the car inside the gates in the charge of a gardener. The house was thatched, and had latticed windows. A crazy paving, with moss growing in between the crevices, led to the front door. The path was bordered with daffodils where the grass grew long. Cherry trees, heavy with pink blossom, a bush of lavender and hollyhocks, purple clematis against the cream walls, and the sweet perfume of honeysuckle — all these Miss Frayle noted with dreamy content. There was a dovecote, too, and a grassy avenue between a line of old oak trees.

'It's like a picture. Almost too good to be true,' she sighed. Then she caught the Doctor's arm. 'Oh, just look! Over there through the trees! It's a mound of earth with bluebells growing round it, and there's a marble cross on the top.'

'The grave of the late Mrs. Hopbridge,' he murmured. 'She committed felo de se two years ago, regrettably as the result of delirium after a recurrence of fever which she contracted while she was in the tropics, where she was accompanying Mr. Hopbridge on one of his archeological expeditions.'

'How sad. It must have been a terrible blow for poor Mr. Hopbridge.'

'It was, indeed. They were a devoted couple. However, he bore his loss with fortitude, and I have no doubt he would not wish his bereavement to cloud the enjoyment of our visit.' She dragged her gaze away from the grave. 'It is certainly a beautiful spot.'

Hopbridge came to the door to greet them. A powerfully built man in the prime of life, his step was springy, his complexion fresh and tanned. Slight shadows under his eyes were the only indication that he had ever known grief. His cheerful, bluff manner did not show it.

'My dear Doctor Morelle!' Shaking the Doctor's hand with sincere vigour. 'Grand to see you! Something like old times!' He enveloped Miss Frayle's hand with both of his. 'And this will be Miss Frayle — almost as famous as the celebrated Doctor, eh?'

She blushed with becoming modesty, and felt a pleasurable glow of importance

'Come right in,' their host invited. 'My housekeeper is already preparing tea. Now you are free to do just as you like here. Go to bed as early or late as you like. Get up at any old time. Ramble off on your own, if you want, or borrow bicycles from the shed. We don't stand on ceremony or convention here. Just enjoy yourselves.'

'That we shall indubitably do. Miss

Frayle, and I have been anticipating this weekend with distinct pleasure.'

Hopbridge's excellence as a host was even more evident when Miss Frayle went up to the sunny room allotted to the Doctor, to unpack his suitcase. There was an ashtray and a small silver box containing the Doctor's very exclusive brand of cigarettes — yes, the inevitable Le Sphinx. On a table beside the bed were the latest books in their shining new covers. In her own room — a little smaller than the Doctor's but equally pleasant — she discovered a box of chocolates and a bottle of boiled sweets; also an assortment of the latest novels — detective and romantic, as though her host had been undecided exactly which form of escapism would be most attractive to her. As a considerate afterthought, there were current copies of the latest woman's magazines.

After dinner Miss Frayle strolled round the grounds. When she came back she discovered the Doctor and their host enjoying themselves over a game of bezique.

Doctor Morelle retired to bed at nine-thirty, knowing he would not offend his host by so doing. Shortly afterwards Miss Frayle, too, bade goodnight, and in her room, leisurely and luxuriously prepared herself for bed. She lay reading one of the novels provided, and munched a chocolate. 'It doesn't matter how late I read,' she soliloquised recklessly, 'I haven't any work to do tomorrow, and I can stay in bed as long as I like!'

She heard the church clock toll midnight before she clicked out the light and, turning on her right side, drifted into an easy sleep. The unaccustomed quiet woke her at what must have been two o'clock; she heard the church clock strike twice. She listened idly to the silence, and gradually picked out individual sounds — the soft wind in the trees, the distant sound of a train and a dog barking afar off. Then she heard the snapping of twigs and — was it imagination? — heavy footsteps on the crazy paving. She wriggled out of bed and walked to the window, pulling back the curtain so that the moonlight streamed in her eyes.

Quickly she drew back. Walking across the lawn towards the avenue of trees she saw — 'Mr. Hopbridge!'

She watched him making his way towards the avenue of oak trees. She thought for a moment: 'He's going to his wife's grave — some moonlight tryst or something. Oh, poor man!' But he branched off before he came to the white cross that shone in the moonlight, and just disappeared into the shadows.

She waited at the window for a quarter of an hour, and did not see him return. Puzzled, she snuggled back into her bed.

Next morning she was surprised to find that her host had been downstairs a full hour before she came down, despite his perambulations in the small hours.

She couldn't contain her curiosity, and as she greeted him she searchingly added: 'It was a heavenly moon last night, wasn't it? I nearly joined you in your stroll as the church clock chimed two.'

He appeared to start. She noticed that his manner was slightly agitated, and his eyes heavy with tiredness.

'I'm afraid I must have disturbed you,

Miss Frayle,' he said at last. 'You see I am rather apt to take my exercise at all hours of the night.' His voice dropped in timbre. 'For the past two years, I've found that I need very little sleep.'

Miss Frayle would gladly have bitten off her tongue. She had indeed made a faux pas. He had evidently suffered from insomnia since his wife's death.

A few minutes later the Doctor joined them, and they all sat down to breakfast together. The housekeeper and the parlourmaid served, and Miss Frayle could not help but notice there was something strained about their manner; something inexplicable that cast a sinister air of foreboding over the room. Heavy storm clouds gathered outside and seemed to add to the eeriness of the atmosphere.

As she was about to depart with a tray, the thin-lipped housekeeper turned to Hopbridge and burst out:

'I don't think it's right that you don't tell Doctor Morelle about the 'appening. If anyone can 'elp us, 'e can. None of us will feel safe in our beds unless something's done!'

With that she disappeared through the doorway.

The Doctor drained his coffee. He glanced at Hopbridge: 'Am I to deduce from your domestic's impassioned peroration that you are hiding something from me?'

The other stroked his chin evasively. 'As a matter of fact, there is something I intended to keep dark, y'see, if that fool of a housekeeper hadn't blurted it out, I didn't want you to be disturbed on your quiet weekend.'

'Considerate of you. Nevertheless, I would like to know what has transpired.'

'It's a rather shocking affair, really. Our local Vicar's been found dead in the Vicarage study early this morning. His head was battered in!'

'What!' Miss Frayle somersaulted her grapefruit. 'Oh, that's a terrible thing to happen.'

'Two or three hundred pounds were taken from his safe, so it looks like a nasty case of murder.'

The Doctor sighed wearily. 'Could you pour me some more coffee, Miss Frayle?'

he asked at a tangent. 'Must be somewhat of a shock to you,' he said to Hopbridge. 'Were you well acquainted with the reverend gentleman?'

'I knew him quite well. Can't say I feel any grief over the fellow. We weren't — well, we weren't on very good terms together. Y'see, after my wife's death he refused to let her be buried in the churchyard — on hallowed ground. Never quite forgave him for that.'

The Doctor nodded his head contemplatively. 'Did you not mention to me recently something concerning an apparition which was popularly supposed to haunt the churchyard to which the Vicarage is adjacent?'

Miss Frayle almost dropped the coffee pot as she gasped: 'Oh a ghost too!'

Doctor Morelle turned on her with quick irritation. 'I prefer to partake of the coffee from the cup, Miss Frayle!' he exclaimed tartly. 'It is quite unnecessary to slop it into the saucer.'

'Sorry, Doctor,' she said, holding his cup in trembling hands. 'There you are.'

'A ghost?' their host was echoing. 'Yes,

that's quite true. You wouldn't get any of the villagers to walk through the church-yard at night for a fortune.'

'Nor me either!' Miss Frayle breathed fervently.

Hopbridge smoothed his hair. 'No doubt,' he remarked, 'the death of the Vicar will be put down to the ghost by most of the folk round here.'

Doctor Morelle chuckled sardonically. 'And yet the plundering of the victim's safe would seem to give body to a more material type of assailant!'

The other shook his head. 'Not in the minds of these country folk,' he asserted. 'I tell you superstition dies hard in this part of the world.'

The Doctor rose from the table and walked to the window, lighting a Le Sphinx thoughtfully.

'Well, it is an appropriately cloudy and dismal morning; shall you and I, my dear Miss Frayle, take a stroll through this haunted churchyard and perhaps call in at the scene of the crime?'

'Don't — don't you think it looks as if it might come on to rain?' she suggested, not relishing the idea of leaving the bright morning room for a dismal, haunted churchyard.

'Not a bit, not a bit.' He dismissed the weather peremptorily. 'I feel positive the elements will hold long enough for you and I to undertake the little expedition I have suggested.'

'I'm sure it's going to pour.'

'No, I think you'll be all right,' Hopbridge assured her. 'Look! There's a tiny patch of blue sky over there.'

'What a pity!' she groaned.

The Doctor was saying:

'Merely as a precautionary measure, you might be good enough to fetch me my mackintosh.' As she hurried out of the room in search of the garment, he turned to the other. 'Tell me how we go, through the village, do we not, and then bear — '

'You *can* go that way. But there's a much shorter cut. You go straight through the avenue of oak trees in my grounds, through a wicket gate at the end of the path and into a little wood. Then you'll see the church ahead of you, with the Vicarage beside it.'

A quarter of an hour later, as they were pushing through the wicket gate, Miss Frayle told the Doctor how she had seen their host wandering in that direction at two o'clock in the morning.

'I don't know what to make of it,' she pondered. 'You don't think that he — that he — ?'

'I have long since suspected him as an insomniac,' he said evasively, and added: 'At this juncture, Miss Frayle, perhaps it would be more prudent if you do not mention to anyone what you observed.'

'Yes, Doctor — I understand. But I knew it was all right to tell you.'

'Quite right.'

She stumbled through the thicket a few yards behind him. They rounded a clump of trees, and ahead of them lay the church.

'What a dear little church!' she rhapsodised. 'It's so rustic isn't it, Doctor Morelle?'

'The square tower and general architecture would seem to proclaim it as being of the Norman Conquest era,' he speculated.

'It looks awfully old. Isn't there always

a peculiar smell in churchyards? Particularly after rain; a smell of newly dug clay or something,' she pondered. 'The place doesn't really look frightening now — but at night, with that clock chiming and these old trees — ' She shuddered. 'I could just imagine the ghost coming from behind that big tombstone, and floating down this path and walking right *through* this gate and — '

She broke off with a little scream and caught his arm, for hardly had she spoken than a figure actually did appear in sight behind the large tombstone.

'Look! Oh, Doctor!' she fluttered, 'it's coming towards us!'

He compressed his lips impatiently. 'Miss Frayle, if only you would make an effort to focus your astigmatic vision accurately you would perceive that this figure, far from being a spirit materialisation, is an extremely normal and earthy male specimen. I would deduce that the man's forbears were agricultural labourers, and that this man has now evolved into an artisan, although indubitably he still retains the feudal feelings of a person who has been reared on the land.'

'He's coming through the gate!' she said breathlessly.

'But *not* without opening it, my dear Miss Frayle!' he chuckled.

The newcomer looked up at them and smiled in the friendly manner of country folk.

'Good morning, miss,' he greeted with a rich burr, touching his cap. 'Good morning, sir.'

Doctor Morelle inclined his head, and Miss Frayle returned the man's respectful greeting.

'Be terrible about the Reverend Vicar, baint it?' the man said in awed tones. He removed his cap, and turned it in his thick, strong hands. 'This be a quiet place — nothing terrible happened like this afore. Sad it be — the pore Vicar — and me having just this morning got the church organ all fixed up with electricity, too.'

The Doctor's eyes narrowed. 'I take it you are the village electrician?'

The man chewed at his moustache. 'That I be,' he nodded. 'And I promised the Reverend Vicar last night the organ'd be ready for him to hear it today. Had his heart set on having it electrified. The organ used to be worked by bellows, ye see.'

Miss Frayle murmured something sympathetically

The man shook his head. 'And there it be, all ready for him and he lying there, dead. My, it be a sad day for the village. I reckon the ghost took his revenge on the poor Reverend for bringing such a modern idea into the old church, I do. Ay.'

'That is as may be,' the Doctor conceded. 'But it has so transpired that while taking its revenge the — er — ghost appropriated the contents of the Vicarage safe!' Watching the workman closely he added: 'No doubt the person who committed the crime was simple-minded and expected this superstitious balderdash to provide him with an effective alibi.'

The workman touched his nicotine-stained moustache and his grey eyes appeared blank. 'Those be big words you use, sir, words furrin to these parts.' He turned his bleak gaze to the Vicarage where the curtains and blinds were drawn over the windows. 'Pore man, and the church organ what he'd set his heart on having electrified waiting for him to hear for the first time and he won't never hear a note of it.'

Miss Frayle's eyes glistened sympathetically.

'It's very sad,' she murmured in a suitably hushed tone.

'Ay, that it be.' The man replaced his cap. 'Well, good-day to you, sir and miss. Good-day, though it do look like it's going to rain buckets pretty soon, good-day!' He shuffled down the lane murmuring, 'Ay, poor Reverend Vicar won't never hear a note of it.'

Miss Frayle watched the receding figure with a puzzled frown.

'Well, what do you make of that, Doctor?' she asked

He examined the end of his cigarette attentively.

'I gathered,' he remarked at last, 'from what he said he has this morning completed the conversion of the church organ from the hand-blown bellows type to that of the electrically-driven kind.'

Her face brightened like that of a puzzled child who at last knows the answer to its teacher's question. 'You mean it used to be worked by hand and now it's done by electricity?'

He gazed at her with mock credulity. 'I am amazed by the rapidity with which your mind absorbs ideas, Miss Frayle!'

She decided to be unabashed.

'Didn't you think that there was a rather — well, a rather *shifty* look in that workman's eyes?' she queried. 'Almost as though he had something to *hide*!'

He clicked his tongue impatiently.

'And his grief, too,' she puzzled, 'don't you think that was a little over-done?'

'Really, your feminine speculations and deductions are most exasperating,' he admonished. 'Whenever we are presented with a problem, why must you always be preoccupied with externals — with futile details of reactions. No murderer has ever been found guilty, simply because he *appeared* to be suspicious. Admittedly, actions that have a suspicious motive may strengthen the case where the evidence is purely circumstantial. But in all the cases we have investigated the deduction has been arrived at through scientific rationalisation, the finding of that inevitable and usually material error — admittedly sometimes difficult to discover by anyone except myself, but nevertheless an error which is existent, to those who have eyes to perceive.'

'I think I understand, Doctor.'

'I certainly wish you would endeavour to do so. Quite succinctly I have given you the whole key to crime detection. Later, when we have completed our investigation — ' he took a long draw at his cigarette, 'I will give you the opportunity to solve this case yourself.'

Miss Frayle goggled excitedly. 'That is going to be thrilling. Oh, I do wish I'd brought my notebook.'

'For what, pray?'

'To write down all the clues and things. My shorthand is very quick, and I — I could scribble down everything people said.'

'And no doubt strike everyone mute in the process!'

'But — oh dear, there are so many things to remember,' she flustered. 'Tell me, have — have there been any material clues so far?'

'If I informed you, wouldn't that be making your task rather too simple?'

She pouted. 'It isn't fair,' she exclaimed. 'You're always hinting that I'm not nearly as clever as you are — '

'And now you have the opportunity of proving the reverse,' he chuckled. 'I cannot imagine anything fairer.'

'All right then! If you say so,' she agreed dubiously. 'Well, where do we go from here?'

She broke off, and stood quite still with her eyes round like saucers and her mouth open. The strains of an organ were coming from the church. The melody was elusive, almost indiscernible at the outset, then gradually it grew to a clamorous crescendo. It was no known music. It was an improvisation, eerie, bizarre and macabre — a wailing and agonised cacophony, yet through it ran a certain musical sequence.

The Doctor dropped his Le Sphinx in the lane and pressed his toe to the glowing end.

'I think from here we will proceed to the church,' he decided. 'Our village electrician seems to have performed the operation adequately. Let us hear it at closer range.'

'It gives me the creeps,' she shivered. 'That music! It's so — so weird!'

'Come, Miss Frayle. You are in charge of the investigations, are you not?'

'Me! Oh dear — I don't know whether I feel like it. I tell you what, Doctor, I'll take on your *next* case.'

'I fear you will not have the opportunity,' he pointed out laconically. 'Come, lead on.'

She was careful to see she was only one foot ahead of him. The double doors of the church were ajar, and they entered noiselessly. To the right of the altar was the organ with its graduated bronze pipes leading high to the roof of the church. She caught the side view of the man playing the instrument.

'Look, he's wearing queer, dark glasses,' she breathed, and she stood fascinated, watching the organist's tall lean frame swaying in a frenzy of neurotic ecstasy as he plunged at the keyboards. She noticed the man's high bony forehead, and the raven darkness of his hair, which accentuated his curiously aesthetic pallor.

'Let us approach nearer the organist,' Doctor Morelle said softly. 'No doubt you would like to make some enquiries.'

'What? Me!' she flurried. 'I wouldn't know what to ask him.'

'Very well, then I will interrogate him,' he agreed, 'and you will listen closely for clues, will you not?'

'Oh yes, I'll do that.'

He walked swiftly down the aisle. He stood beside the organist, who observed him from the corners of his eyes, and studiously went on playing for a few bars before he pushed in the stops and clicked off the switch which controlled the electric bellows.

The Doctor bowed slightly. 'I must apologise for interrupting your performance.'

'Ah, good morning — 'The man spoke in a slow and sombre voice. 'I don't think we have met — '

'I am Doctor Morelle, and this is my assistant, Miss Frayle. And you are, I gather, the church organist?'

'Yes, I am the organist,' the man intoned. 'My name is Lake — Ebenezer Lake. I have just been testing the new electrical device which works the instrument.'

The Doctor nodded understandingly. 'And you find it an improvement, no doubt?' he queried.

Lake's thin lips tightened. 'That is not for me to say,' he replied enigmatically, and his features assumed the expression of a person who has many things to deplore.

'But why not, pray? Surely you are the best judge?'

The man turned his dark lenses full on the Doctor. 'It was not my wish to change something which has obtained here for hundreds of years. I am not alone, either, in my disagreement.'

'Who else is there who disagrees with this innovation?'

The man rose. It seemed as though he towered above them. He pointed a gaunt hand in the direction of the churchyard.

'The phantom that struck down the Vicar,' he announced sombrely.

'Come now, surely you don't believe that legend.'

The man averted his head and glanced at the church door.

'I was here last night, alone,' he began in awed tones. 'Yes, I was playing this organ as I have been used to doing. I was playing it for the last time before it was — modernised! Then a strange feeling came over me. I had the feeling that I was not alone. Can you understand that?'

'*I* can,' Miss Frayle exclaimed with a shudder. 'What happened then?'

'A strong premonition seized me. Almost against my own will I broke off the music, and I found myself walking towards the window. That one over there.' Again the man pointed dramatically. 'I looked out — '

'Yes! Yes!' she gasped breathlessly.

'I saw a grey figure floating through the churchyard towards the vicarage.'

'Was — was it a man or a woman?' queried Miss Frayle tensely, remembering their host's dead wife. Surely, she thought, it would be logical that Mrs. Hopbridge might haunt the churchyard where the Vicar refused her burial.

'A female figure?' the organist echoed. 'That I cannot say. It was not human. The apparition, as I watched, went towards the Vicarage and — ' he broke off as he saw the Doctor yawning sceptically. With dignity he said: 'But I see, by your expression, my story does not convince you.'

'Oh, but it does,' broke in Miss Frayle, on tenterhooks.

'I fear not,' the man murmured. 'Now if you will excuse me, I must continue with my playing.'

Doctor Morelle gave the organist a penetrating look. 'It is unfortunate you had no witness here with you who — er — might have corroborated your ghost story.'

The man started almost imperceptibly, then a superior smile quirked the corners of his thin lips.

'I was quite alone. Already I have told you that. Strangers to the village do not understand.' He intoned slowly, 'There are old spirits haunting the place — spirits who resent changes. They loathe — ' he drew out the word — 'they loathe that the things they have known for many years should be disturbed.'

He began playing the organ softly.

Doctor Morelle signalled to Miss Frayle. 'Come. The door here leads to the vestry, I presume, and from there we will be able to leave the church.'

He closed the vestry door after them. Immediately she turned to him.

'Doctor, why did you upset him like that?' she asked in puzzlement. 'I was watching for clues, and I'm sure he was just going to give us some useful information. I can't think why you didn't pretend to believe — '

'And I cannot imagine why you, Miss Frayle, had not the foresight to bring an umbrella. It is about to rain heavily, and I shall become saturated.'

'On the contrary,' she announced triumphantly. 'I have brought an umbrella.'

'Indeed. I do not perceive it.'

'It's a chubby one,' she exclaimed. 'Fits in the inside pocket of my mac. See!'

'Highly ingenious,' he commented. 'But I fail to see how such a diminutive article could be utilitarian. Merely a feminine fancy, I presume. However, I will take charge of it.'

'But you won't be able to open it. You have to have the knack of it,' she pointed out.

'I do not need to open it,' he said tersely.

'I don't understand,' she puzzled.

'No doubt you soon will.'

'Anyway,' she said resignedly, 'we can shelter here until the heavy downpour stops.'

'On the contrary, I should have thought that you would wish to proceed to the local police station forthwith. No time should be lost.'

'Why — why should I want to go to the police station? Whatever for — ?'

He gave a slow smile of condescension. 'Merely to advise the officer in charge of an important discovery you have no doubt made relating to the mystery of the Vicar's demise.'

'I haven't made any discovery,' she protested. 'Just as I was getting on to a clue, you snubbed the organist and — '

He raised his eyebrows in mock surprise. 'Am I to assume you have not elucidated the mystery? Really, Miss Frayle, your limited powers of deduction amaze me. If you hadn't been so enthralled by Mr. Lake's sensational and superstitious farrago, you might have discovered that he virtually confessed to murdering the poor Vicar — '

'How could you know?' she gasped. 'It's beyond me. Why — ' she broke off. 'Listen! Oh, Doctor, he's stopped playing — '

'That I perceived forty-five seconds ago.' He now spoke quickly, urgently. 'Proceed to the corner of the vestry. Do not move.'

She put a trembling hand to her mouth as she saw the vestry door being opened slowly. The Doctor stood a little to the left of the door, his hands clasped behind him. A dark figure loomed in the doorway

— Ebenezer Lake. A shrill scream broke from her lips as she saw Lake was menacingly holding a weighted life-preserver.

Lake lumbered forward.

'No, Doctor Clever-Morelle, you are not going to the police station,' he snarled. 'Instead you are going to join the Vicar — you and the young lady.'

Her attempt at a scream was now only a mouse-like squeak.

'Think you're smart, don't you?' Lake challenged. 'Think you can come to our village and poke your nose into things that don't concern you — '

'Look out, Doctor!' Miss Frayle shouted frenziedly.

Lake raised the life-preserver aloft, and brought it crashing down. Miss Frayle crouched in the corner, putting her hands in front of her eyes. She heard the crash of a weapon on a human skull. Sickeningly, too, she heard an agonised groan and a body falling to the floor.

'Doctor Morelle!' she screamed. 'And I'm next! Oh dear, oh dear — !'

Then she heard a soft voice say:

'What is it, my dear Miss Frayle?' followed by a sardonic laugh. Unmistakably it was Doctor Morelle's voice and laugh. Or was — was it his ghost? She opened her fingers slightly and peered through.

The Doctor, quite unhurt, was standing in front of her, a slight smile on his calm features.

'Your solicitude for my well-being was indeed touching,' he murmured, 'even though in the next breath it was qualified by anxiety for your own safety.'

'Oh, Doctor, you're all right. Thank heavens!' She clutched at his arms in relief. 'What — what happened?'

'Perceive Lake lying recumbent — stunned, I fear.'

Her eyes goggled in admiration.

'Doctor, you're wonderful! How did you do it?'

He gave an over-elaborate smile of self-deprecation.

'Merely a judicious sidestep,' he murmured calmly, 'and then your umbrella proved more utilitarian than I had imagined.'

'I'm glad I remembered that umbrella, particularly as you didn't bring your swordstick on the holiday . . . Holiday!' She gave a laugh. 'Funny sort of holiday! Hasn't been a very quiet time for you, what with one thing and another — '

He raised his right hand to cut her short.

'Pray subdue your nervous chatter and proceed with all expediency to fetch police assistance while I stand guard over this — er — gentleman.' He added: 'You may take my mackintosh to protect you from the elements. Hurry now, hurry.'

★   ★   ★

It was after lunch. Hopbridge warmed his balloon brandy glass in his hands and regarded Doctor Morelle with friendly admiration.

'Must hand it to you, Doctor,' he beamed. 'Between breakfast and lunch you solve a murder which would have kept our local police scratching their skulls for weeks.' He raised his glass 'Here's to you!'

The Doctor inclined his head at the tribute. 'It was simplicity itself,' he murmured.

Miss Frayle uncurled herself from the armchair.

'But you haven't yet told us how you knew Lake was the murderer,' she pointed out. 'I'm dying to know.'

'Yes, Doctor, let's have it,' Hopbridge grinned. 'Must confess it's got me beat.'

'Very well, I'll tell you — but just a moment, Miss Frayle; before I commence, it might not be amiss if you would kindly write down my words in order to complete the account of the case for a chapter in my future memoirs — '

Hopbridge handed Miss Frayle some notepaper and his own silver pencil.

'Ready, Doctor,' she signalled with her poised pencil. Fluently and in an even voice he began his dictation. The others hung on every word:

'The important discovery I made,' said Doctor Morelle levelly, 'was that the church organist's story consisted of deliberate fabrication. This postulated that he possessed some vital knowledge concerning the murder of the Vicar. As it transpired he was, in fact the murderer — having been surprised by his victim while in the act of robbing his safe. Had he not stated he was playing the church organ *alone* (in italics, please, Miss Frayle), that night, he might have escaped with his crime. The organ, however, was not then driven by electricity, but by bellows which necessitated the presence of another person to operate.'

'Well. I never — ' gasped Miss Frayle. 'Why didn't I think of that?'

'Why, indeed?'

She nibbled the end of the silver pencil, then hurriedly removed it from her teeth as she realised it belonged to their host.

'Anything more to finish off the chapter, Doctor?'

'Well, I — er I — yes, one of course needs to close on some appropriate note,' he pondered, drawing at his Le Sphinx. 'I cannot quite think of a suitable — '

'I know,' prompted Miss Frayle sweetly. 'We could end with something modest and unassuming about yourself, Doctor. About your inimitable deductive gifts, brilliant methods of criminal investigation, amazingly penetrating mind, colossal powers of — '

He nodded seriously.

'Very well,' he agreed, 'let us conclude the chapter along these lines you suggest.' His tone changed as he detected an impish twinkle behind Miss Frayle's spectacles. 'Er — Miss Frayle!'

'Yes, Doctor Morelle?' she asked innocently.

His tone was deeply pained. 'I am inclined to suspect that you were being sarcastic and sardonically humorous at my expense.'

'Oh no — ' She tried hard to stop the quivering of her lips.

'It is a trait in your manner which I can view only with the greatest abhorrence,' he admonished. 'You really must try to correct such an unpleasant characteristic and cultivate a manner more considerate and kindly.'

Hopbridge burst into hearty laughter.

'Take it easy, Doctor,' he advised. 'The little lady certainly put one over on you there. Where's your sense of humour?'

The Doctor turned to him with a shocked and amazed expression, as though he were thinking: 'Et tu Brute?'

Then the strained atmosphere suddenly snapped. Doctor Morelle's lips curled upwards and he laughed too — and soon the room echoed with the laughter of all three of them.

'Nothing like a few days' rest for making a man see the funny side of things,' Hopbridge observed. 'Let's go for a walk. The weather's clearing up.'

4

The Case of the Portable Typewriter

In the course of his long and varied career Doctor Morelle was not infrequently called into consultation by other medical men who wished to enjoy the advantage of his specialised knowledge on various psychological aspects of disease. To the ordinary public he might be best known as a highly successful criminologist; but to himself his work in the world of crime was merely a sideline albeit an interesting one, of a life devoted to science.

There were occasions, however, when even his acute and detailed knowledge of the various aspects of medicine and psychology did not suffice. Then he was wont to call into consultation some expert in another branch of science.

On one such occasion the Doctor was staying at the country house of Sir

Bertram Harper, the celebrated anthropologist, since he wished to consult that great man on the anthropological aspects of brain development, on which he was preparing a paper to be delivered at a forthcoming session of the British Association for the Advancement of Science.

Sir Bertram had proved very helpful, and had himself made the suggestion that Doctor Morelle should come to stay with him, the more especially since the house contained an extensive library of books on anthropological topics which would give the two men all the references needed for a closely reasoned paper such as that which Doctor Morelle was preparing.

Miss Frayle accompanied the Doctor, since he knew that he would have to do a good deal of dictation during his stay, the bulk of the paper having to be written during the weekend.

One evening the Doctor and Sir Bertram Harper lingered after dinner, savouring a glass apiece of the very excellent port which Sir Bertram, a connoisseur of wine, invariably provided for his distinguished guests.

The maid came in: 'I'm sorry, Sir Bertram,' she said, 'but you are wanted on the telephone,'

Sir Bertram looked faintly annoyed. He liked the ancient ritual of the port, and he objected to any sort of interruption to that rite.

'Did you tell him that it was difficult, and that I was not to be disturbed, being in conference with Doctor Morelle on scientific matters?' he asked.

'I did, Sir Bertram,' replied the maid.

'And what did the caller say?'

The maid looked a little confused for a moment, as if she found it difficult to transpose the caller's reply into reasonably polite terms.

'He said that he would still have to ask you to come to the 'phone, as it was a very urgent matter, which could not wait,' the maid said.

Sir Bertram shrugged his shoulders in a gesture of mute resignation.

'Very well,' he said. 'I shall have to accept the call, I suppose. If you will be so kind as to excuse me for a brief time, Doctor Morelle?'

'Naturally,' the Doctor replied. 'On an occasion such as this one naturally does one's best to assist, It is clearly a matter of some considerable urgency if your caller insists on interrupting what he has been told is an important scientific consultation. No one could possibly want to stand in the way on such an occasion,'

With a pleasant nod and a smile, Sir Bertram left the room. The Doctor sipped his port in meditative fashion, and waited, without any outward sign of impatience, the return of his host.

He was surprised when Sir Bertram returned. The man's ruddy countenance had perceptibly paled, He was breathing quickly in an agitated manner, and it was clear enough that the telephone conversation had considerably disturbed him.

'I trust that your news on the telephone was in no way disturbing Sir Bertram?' the Doctor said.

'It was very disturbing, I'm afraid, Doctor,' replied Sir Bertram.

Miss Frayle, who, as the only lady present, had been allowed to stay during the male ritual of drinking the port, looked a trifle alarmed.

'Yes,' Sir Bertram went on, 'Something dreadful has happened. An old friend of mine — Harry Bell by name — has been found shot dead.'

'Oh, how awful, Sir Bertram!' Miss Frayle exclaimed, her hand on her heart.

'I am indeed extremely distressed to hear such sad news,' said Doctor Morelle gravely.

'That was the local Inspector of Police on the 'phone,' Sir Bertram explained. 'I was Harry's closest friend, and he wants me to go over there at once. They think that I might be able to help — though in what way I can't for the life of me imagine. Still, the house is not far away, and it is not the sort of request which one can well refuse.'

'Was the cause of death accidental?' inquired Doctor Morelle.

Sir Bertram Harper shook his head solemnly, 'No,' he said. 'I'm very much afraid that it looks like suicide. Apparently Harry left a farewell note behind.' He paused for a moment, as if he was a little uncertain how to phrase his next remark. Then he said: 'I wonder if you'd care to come over with me, Doctor. You have more knowledge of this sort of thing than I have, and I'd much appreciate it if you would come.'

'Certainly I will come with you,' the Doctor agreed readily enough. 'Although, from what you have said, it would appear that there is very little that I can do to help.'

Miss Frayle looked up brightly, 'Shall I come along as well, Doctor?' she asked.

Doctor Morelle smiled sardonically, 'I imagine that your query is merely rhetorical, Miss Frayle,' he remarked. 'After all, you must realise how invaluable to me your presence is on these sad and dramatic occasions.'

'Thank you, Doctor,' replied Miss Frayle, blushing at the unusual and totally unexpected compliment.

Sir Bertram made his way slowly to the door, 'Poor chap!' he murmured to himself, 'I never realised that he was in much desperate straits. The last time I saw him . . . ' It appeared that the anthropologist realised that he had been speaking his thoughts aloud, and he stopped, turning to the Doctor. 'I'll tell them to get the car out,' he said. 'And then, as soon as you're ready, Doctor, we will be off.'

'We will be at your disposal in approximately three minutes,' Doctor Morelle said. 'It is only necessary for me to get a hat and coat, and for Miss Frayle to perform those mysterious matters with a powder-puff which the ladies seem to regard as necessary for all occasions, whether they be happy or tragic ones.'

It was, indeed, less than five minutes before they were all seated in Sir Bertram Harper's massive Lagonda saloon, purring smoothly over the two or three miles of country road which separated Sir Bertram's house from that of his friend, Harry Bell.

Mr. Bell's house was a pleasant little villa, situated in neatly laid-out gardens. As soon as they arrived a solemn manservant ushered them into the presence of the Inspector who had previously spoken to Sir Bertram on the 'phone.

'I'm very sorry about this, Sir Bertram,'

he said. 'It must have come as a dreadful shock to you. But you were poor Mr. Bell's nearest friend, and I thought that it would be a good plan for you to come over at once. You might be able, perhaps, to be of some assistance to us.'

Sir Bertram looked distressed, indeed, but he waved aside the Inspector's apologies. 'Of course, Inspector, of course,' he said. 'Anything that I can do to help in this sad affair I shall be only too pleased to do. I have brought over Doctor Morelle and Miss Frayle, who are staying with me. The Doctor has some considerable experience of tragic events of one sort and another, and he may be able to offer us some helpful advice in the situation which has arisen here.'

'How do you do, Doctor?' the Inspector said politely, not registering either approval or disapproval of the presence of these unexpected visitors. 'How do you do, Miss Frayle?'

'How do you do, Inspector?' Miss Frayle replied, but the Doctor said nothing, apparently regarding anything in the nature of social conversation as mere

118

time wasting when there was a mysterious death awaiting investigation.

'The body,' the Inspector began, and then paused, 'Mr. Bell, I should say,' he added, 'is in the library. Would you be so kind as to come this way.'

He walked down the corridor, and the others followed him, Doctor Morelle noted that the house was elaborately furnished. Whatever might be the reason for the presumed suicide, it was extremely unlikely that financial worries could be behind it, since there was every indication of comfort, if not of immense wealth.

In the library the Doctor at once made a cursory examination of the body.

'Hm!' he murmured. 'There seems to be little doubt that the wounds were inflicted with a shotgun. Where did you find the weapon, Inspector?'

'Here, by the body, Doctor,' the Inspector said, indicating a place on the floor. 'Those chalk-marks on the floor show where it was.'

Doctor Morelle looked at the spot with interest, and glanced rapidly around the room.

'I presume this would be it on the table,' the Doctor said thoughtfully. 'Sporting rifle, single barrel. You have, of course, examined it for the possible presence of fingerprints, which would give us an indication of what happened?'

'Only Mr. Bell's prints on it, Doctor,' the Inspector said, 'Not a trace of anyone else's.'

Miss Frayle had been looking around the room, while this conversation was going on. She resolutely averted her eyes from the body, and concentrated her attention on other parts of the library.

'This is the note which he left, I suppose,' she said at length, indicating a piece of paper on the desk.

'That is it, Miss,' agreed the Inspector.

'I wonder why he typed it in capitals?' she mused. Then she read it aloud: 'IT'S NO USE TRYING TO CARRY ON ANY MORE, I'VE DONE MY BEST, BUT I CAN'T, GOODBYE.'

'That is all he said?' Doctor Morelle inquired.

'Yes,' said Miss Frayle, 'Come and see, Doctor.'

The Doctor strode over to the side of the desk, and looked at the suicide note with every indication of interest.

'Unsigned by the deceased, I see,' he remarked, He paused, his brow wrinkled in puzzlement. Then he turned suddenly to the Inspector, and asked: 'Inspector, who first discovered that the tragedy had taken place?'

'Mr. Bell's manservant, the fellow who let you in when you arrived here, He's called Fowler.'

'He seemed a very pleasant man,' Miss Frayle remarked.

'He seems all right to me, too,' answered the Inspector. 'He's a bit upset, naturally, at what has happened. He can't throw much light on the business, but if you would like to have a chat with him, I'll send him in to you.'

'I could bear to have converse with him,' Doctor Morelle announced thoughtfully.

'Right,' the Inspector said.

Sir Bertram had been silent for sometime and now he said, in a somewhat faint voice: 'I think, if you will excuse me, I should like to sit down somewhere quietly for a few minutes. This has all been a bit of a shock to me, and I should like to have the opportunity of getting over it by myself.' The famous anthropologist did, indeed, look almost all in. His normally tanned face had taken on an unhealthy pallor, and there was a quiver in his voice, which gave a good indication of the strain under which he was suffering. He slowly walked to the door, keeping his face averted from the mortal remains of his old friend.

'Shall I come with you, Sir Bertram?' asked Miss Frayle solicitously.

'No, no, my dear, thank you,' Sir Bertram replied with a smile of grateful thanks. 'I'll go into the lounge, I think, and sit down. I shall be all right in a few minutes.'

They looked at the man in silence as he walked out. Sir Bertram seemed to have aged years in a matter of a few minutes. There was no doubt that the death of his old friend had been a profound shock to him. And possibly the manner of that death had upset him more than the actual fact of death.

'Fowler is the name of the manservant, Doctor,' said the Inspector when Sir Bertram had gone.

'You mentioned that before, Inspector,' Doctor Morelle replied. 'Would you send him in now, please?'

'I'll get him for you right away,' the Inspector announced quietly. The policeman, indeed, gave an air of quiet efficiency that Miss Frayle, at any rate, found very reassuring.

'Why,' the Doctor asked, when he and Miss Frayle were left alone in the room, 'do you continue to moon over that piece of paper, Miss Frayle?'

'I was just thinking,' Miss Frayle answered tremulously, 'how terribly pathetic . . . '

The Doctor interrupted her in a rasping tone. 'There is nothing to be gained by sentimentalising over what has occurred,' he said. 'Sentimentality, my dear Miss Frayle, is a sickly fog which obscures many a clear-cut issue, clouding the vision of all successful and logical thought.'

Miss Frayle sighed deeply. 'I suppose it is rather like crying over spilt milk,' she admitted.

Doctor Morelle rounded on her savagely. 'Why must you insist on reducing my philosophising to commonplace banalities?' he asked in his most irritated manner.

'Yes,' Miss Frayle agreed brightly. 'I suppose it was a rather foolish remark of mine. After all, it is not exactly milk which had been spilt, is it?'

And for once Doctor Morelle was left without an effective answer, since at this moment Fowler came in. He appeared to be very much perturbed by what had happened, and his face showed every sign of mental disturbance.

'The Inspector said that you wished to see me, sir,' he remarked as he entered.

'Perhaps we shall get some sense out of you!' exclaimed the Doctor, with a savage glare at Miss Frayle. 'You were the deceased's manservant, I understand?'

'Yes, sir,' Fowler replied, and waited in silence for the next question to be asked.

'Can you throw any light on what has taken place today?' asked Doctor Morelle.

'Well,' said Fowler in a hesitant manner, 'I knew that Mr. Bell had been extremely depressed these last few months.'

'Did he give any reason for this state of mind?' asked the Doctor thoughtfully.

'I think that he had been in rather a queer state of mind ever since his wife died,' Fowler explained. 'That was several months ago.'

'Hm.' Doctor Morelle considered this information for a few moments before proceeding. Then he said: 'Who was in the house besides Mr. Bell and yourself?'

'No one, sir.'

'You and he have been living here alone, then?' The Doctor seemed somewhat surprised at this.

'Absolutely alone,' Fowler agreed, 'except for a cook and a daily woman. They both live in the village, and don't live in the house.'

'I see. Were either of them on the premises when the tragedy took place?' Doctor Morelle inquired.

'No, sir. The daily woman goes home after lunch every day, and cook went early, as this is her afternoon off. It is a terrible business, sir, I was just coming into the house when it happened, you see.'

'Coming in?' asked the Doctor. It appeared that this case was giving him more than the usual quota of surprises, for he rarely permitted his voice to possess the tone of amazement that now showed itself.

'Yes, sir. I'd been having a quiet smoke in the kitchen garden — a thing which I often do of an evening, when it's a pleasant one like this — when I heard a shot.'

'Did it sound near?' asked Miss Frayle, her eyes open very wide at these revelations of the background of the tragedy.

'It sounded very loud, Miss,' Fowler replied. 'At first I thought that it was someone shooting rabbits out in the field at the back of the garden, and then I realised that it was too loud for that, I hurried in here, where I'd last seen Mr. Bell a few minutes earlier — and, well, there he was, as you will already have heard from the Inspector.'

Miss Frayle had been listening to all this with great interest but she now showed every sign of agitation. Her eyes blinked rapidly, her glasses slipped down to the extreme tip of her nose, and she grasped the Doctor's arm spasmodically.

'Dr. Morelle!' she muttered almost directly into the Doctor's ear.

'What is it, Miss Frayle?' snapped the Doctor in tones that betrayed his extreme irritation.

'Can I whisper to you for a moment? Over here, by the window?' Still grasping him tightly by the arm, she led the Doctor across the room.

The Doctor obediently followed her. Though he sometimes felt more than a trace of contempt for Miss Frayle's supposed brainwaves, he knew that there were occasions when she had a worthwhile idea. Fowler stood where he was left, scarcely watching the others. It seemed that he had been so much shocked by what had occurred that he no longer took much interest in what was going on.

'Now, Miss Frayle,' the Doctor murmured quietly as they arrived by the window. 'I should like to know exactly what is the meaning of this somewhat untimely interruption of yours. I trust that you have some important information to give me.'

'That typewritten note!' she exclaimed.

'What about it?' the Doctor asked.

'Where's the typewriter?' queried Miss Frayle.

'I beg your pardon, Miss Frayle?'

'I said, where's the typewriter?' Miss Frayle asked. 'There isn't one anywhere here that I can see.'

There was a slight pause while Doctor Morelle thought this over carefully, as was his wont on occasions when he was presented with some new idea.

'I perceive what you are inferring, my dear Miss Frayle,' he murmured at last, 'and I think that I may congratulate you on your unusual percipience on this occasion. We may perhaps interrogate Fowler a little further on this point. Possibly he will be able to assist us in the matter.'

He strode across the room once more to where Fowler was standing, his eyes fixed on one spot on the thick-piled carpet.

'Fowler,' he said.

'Sir?' replied Fowler, almost springing to attention at the resumption of the conversation.

'Pray proceed, Fowler,' the Doctor said. 'You found the deceased with the shotgun by his side.'

'Yes, sir.'

'It was lying on the floor?'

'Yes, sir.'

'And what did you do?' asked the Doctor.

'I saw at a glance that Mr. Bell was dead, and I decided that my obvious duty was to telephone for the police without the least delay,' replied Fowler.

'You touched nothing?' inquired the Doctor.

'I was careful not to touch a thing,' Fowler explained. 'I have often read that one of the great points when any sort of tragedy of this sort occurs is to avoid touching anything. So I left everything just as it was.'

Doctor Morelle smiled. 'Very commendable of you, Fowler,' he said, and paused momentarily. Then he resumed:

'The library seems to be a somewhat unusual place to keep a sporting rifle. Something in the nature of a gunroom would appear to be more usual in a house of this kind.'

Fowler smiled a grim smile. 'Mr. Bell must have taken it out of the gunroom,' he said. 'It was his favourite among all the guns that he possessed. He took it out shooting earlier this evening, as a matter of fact; but he got caught in the rain and had to come back. I cleaned and oiled it before I returned it to the gunroom where it belonged and where it was normally kept. I can't think why it was brought up here.'

Miss Frayle plucked the Doctor's sleeve and murmured in his ear once again. 'Don't forget the typewriter, will you, Doctor?'

'Thank you, Miss Frayle,' Doctor Morelle replied suavely. 'However, I had not forgotten it.' The look of annoyance that accompanied these words was so savage that Miss Frayle found herself momentarily recoiling. However, she soon recovered, and even surprised herself by saying: 'That's right, Doctor!' in tones that almost suggested that she was commending her employer for having wholeheartedly accepted a suggestion evolved within her own fertile brain.

'Fowler!' Doctor Morelle said sharply to the manservant, who seemed to be once more descending into a dream.

'Yes, sir,' Fowler replied, momentarily startled out of the apathy which had been overcoming him.

'You will observe,' said the Doctor, 'that the farewell note left by the deceased was written on a typewriter, which I should guess to be a portable — probably a Remington or an Underwood, though, without comparison with the work of various portable machines, I should not like to swear to the exact type of machine which was used by Mr. Bell.'

'I . . . I know, sir,' replied Fowler in hesitant tones that seemed to Miss Frayle to betray a certain trace of uneasiness in his mind.

'Where, then,' Doctor Morelle challenged, 'may we be able to find the machine in question.'

'The machine, sir?' There was something almost deliberately stupid about Fowler's demeanour now, and Miss Frayle congratulated herself on having spotted a really worthwhile point, which might possibly even lead Doctor Morelle to discovering the exact identity of the man who had either driven Bell to his death, or who had — was such a thing, after all, possible? — perhaps even murdered the unfortunate man.

'Surely you have heard the word 'machine' used to describe a typewriter,' Doctor Morelle said, again becoming extremely irritable at the stupidity of the man who was now under cross-examination.

'Oh, you mean the typewriter,' Fowler replied. 'It was always kept on the writing desk.'

'Over there?' Doctor Morelle indicated the opposite side of the room.

'Yes.'

'And why is it not there now?' Doctor Morelle asked, pursuing his cross-examination with its usual relentless intensity.

'It is, sir.'

'Where?'

'If you will look under the newspaper, sir, I think that you will find it.'

Doctor Morelle strode over to the writing desk in question, whipped off the newspaper indicated by Fowler, to find that a newish Underwood portable typewriter was, indeed, hidden beneath the copy of *The Evening Chronicle*, which had lain there.

'Oh, Doctor!' exclaimed Miss Frayle in tones of the deepest disappointment.

'A brilliant piece of deductive reasoning, my dear Miss Frayle,' commented Doctor Morelle. 'I think that you should be congratulated on the acumen by which you concentrated on a totally unimportant aspect of a case which turns out to be commonplace in the extreme,'

'Commonplace, Doctor?' Miss Frayle gasped incredulously.

'Yes.'

'But I don't understand. Do you mean to say that you accept the idea that Mr. Bell committed suicide?'

Doctor Morelle shook his head decisively.

'I do not accept anything of the sort,

Miss Frayle,' he said, smiling mysteriously.

'But . . . but . . . but I'm afraid that, in that case, I just completely fail to see what you are getting at, Doctor?' Miss Frayle objected. 'If it is a simple case of suicide I do more or less see what has happened, though I cannot imagine what adequate motive Mr. Bell had for doing away with himself. But other explanations just fail to make sense to me. Do you mean that it was an accident of some sort?'

'No, Miss Frayle.' It seemed almost as if the Doctor took a kind of mischievous satisfaction out of puzzling his secretary, a sort of deliberate perversity of humour, which certainly seemed to her singularly unfunny.

'Then do you mean it was murder?'

'Yes.' There was no doubt about the emphasis with which this dramatic monosyllable was delivered.

'But who . . . who . . . ?' Miss Frayle was now quite obviously out of her mental depth.

'If you will kindly cease from this

babbling for a few moments, Miss Frayle,' remarked Doctor Morelle in his most icy tones, 'I hope that I shall be able to do something which will make the matter clear even to a somewhat limited intellect such as that which is possessed by yourself.'

This finally reduced Miss Frayle to silence, though she was still quite clearly puzzled by what was going on.

The Doctor turned to Fowler. 'I should like to thank you, Fowler,' he said, 'for having so neatly revealed to my assistant here the mystery of the whereabouts of the missing typewriter — a matter which had apparently been an obsession with her for some time past. But . . . ' He paused.

'Yes, sir?' queried Fowler expectantly.

'Perhaps you will reveal to me a secret equally mysterious and perhaps more important in connection with the tragedy which is the ostensible reason for my presence in this room at this precise moment.'

Fowler, in his turn, looked somewhat mystified by the way in which the conversation was tending.

He merely said: 'I will do my best, sir, if there is anything which I know and which you consider has a bearing on the fact that Mr. Bell was impelled to take his own life.'

'First, Miss Frayle,' Doctor Morelle said, 'I think that the Inspector should be recalled.'

'Certainly, Doctor.' Miss Frayle dutifully left the room to fetch the Inspector, and returned in a matter of a minute or two, accompanied by that worthy.

'What is all this about, Doctor?' he asked, almost as soon as he entered the room.

'I thought it advisable that you should be present before I put a certain question — not unimportant in its implications — to Fowler, here,' Doctor Morelle explained.

'And what is that question?' asked Fowler aggressively. It was almost the first time that the manservant had shown any sign at all of animation.

'You will answer it?' Doctor Morelle asked.

'If it is possible for me to do so, sir,' replied Fowler, with a return to something like his previous attitude of complete subservience.

'Would you reveal to us your motive for murdering your late employer?'

Fowler gasped. '*I* murdered him?' he asked in incredulous tones. 'Don't talk nonsense, Doctor. You're talking through your hat.'

He threw back his head and roared with laughter. Miss Frayle said afterwards that she had never in her life experienced such an eerie sensation. It was, she said, like cold water trickling down her spine.

With her knowledge of Doctor Morelle and his methods, she was quite sure that Fowler was a murderer, and the spectacle of a murderer laughing at the mere suggestion that a murder had been committed was something which she found more horrible than any of the more superficially dramatic things which she had seen in the course of her long career as amanuensis to the great Doctor Morelle.

'Laugh, if such a matter appears to you

to demand laugher,' Doctor Morelle said grimly. 'Nevertheless, Inspector, I should put this man safely under lock and key without any further delay, if I were you.'

And under lock and key Fowler was duly put, although the Inspector was extremely dubious about the wisdom, or even the legality of such a proceeding. Nevertheless, he was sufficiently impressed by Doctor Morelle's acumen to make him take the step of arresting Fowler on suspicion.

★　★　★

Later that evening, in the Police Station, the Inspector conferred with Doctor Morelle and Miss Frayle.

'Now, Doctor,' he said, 'I've taken your word for it that this man Fowler is a murderer. I've even taken your word for it that a murder has been committed — though I must candidly admit that to me there appears little certainty even on that point. Can you give me enough information to enable me to justify myself to the Chief Constable? It is certain that I shall be put under a pretty drastic cross-examination by the Chief before many hours are past, and if I am to persuade him that I have done the right thing in this case I have to have my answers pretty well pat. Otherwise I shall be for it, I can tell you.'

Doctor Morelle smiled grimly.

'I imagine that you will find that Fowler has some small financial benefit from Mr. Bell's death,' he said. 'Probably he has recently learned that his employer was leaving him a small legacy, as is customary for a comparatively wealthy man with servants who have long been in his employment.'

'That's as it may be, Doctor,' the Inspector said. 'That is, of course, a motive adequate enough for murder. Murder has often been committed for the sake of quite a small sum of money. I am not disputing the existence of a motive. But what I want to know is: What made you suspect that the matter was a murder at all, and not the simple suicide that it seemed to be on the surface?'

'Yes, Doctor,' put in Miss Frayle. 'What

mistake did Fowler make that made you so certain that he was guilty of the crime of killing his employer and benefactor?'

'He gave himself away, as the more clumsy type of criminal invariably does,' the Doctor said in satisfied tones. 'Any person with reasonable powers of logical reasoning and observation would, I think, have noticed the dreadfully obvious blunder which he made during the course of my conversation with him.'

'Was it concerned with the typewriter?' Miss Frayle asked.

'The Doctor rounded on her. My dear Miss Frayle,' he said savagely, 'the typewriter had nothing to do with the crime. It was used by Fowler to type the suicide note merely because it happened to be handy. It was always kept in that room, and it was therefore an obvious tool, ready for his hand.'

'But what was the blunder?' the Inspector asked. He was now quite as puzzled as Miss Frayle.

'Fowler declared to me,' Doctor Morelle said, speaking slowly and choosing his words with care, 'that he had cleaned and oiled the sporting rifle with which his employer had supposedly shot himself. By Fowler's own admission this had taken place only shortly before Mr. Bell's death. Yet you, Inspector, assured me that there were no fingerprints on the gun save those of the dead man himself.'

The Inspector nodded. 'That's so,' he agreed.

'But the manservant's prints should also have been present if his story of cleaning and oiling the gun had been true — that is, unless he had deliberately removed them.'

Miss Frayle looked excited. 'And there was no one else in the house at the time who could possibly have done that, except Fowler himself,' she said.

'Precisely,' agreed Doctor Morelle. 'The possibility of the deceased himself deliberately wiping the firearm before, in fact, committing suicide did occur to me momentarily. But I dismissed such a procedure as being too fantastically far-fetched to be possible in the circumstances.'

Miss Frayle smiled gently. 'It all goes to

show,' she said, 'that you can be too careful about things. Like Fowler, I mean, removing his own fingerprints from the gun to make sure that only the dead man's would be found on the gun.'

'Fortunately for those of us who are comparatively law-abiding,' Doctor Morelle said, 'it would appear that the vast majority of criminals make similar stupid mistakes without for a moment realising that they have done them.'

'It makes you think, doesn't it, Inspector?' Miss Frayle said, as usual giving a stale old platitude the appearance of being a quite new discovery.

Doctor Morelle had the last word. 'If this sordid and complex case has succeeded in causing you to do *that*, Miss Frayle,' he said, 'then it has indeed accomplished something little short of the miraculous.'

5

The Case of the Voice in the Night
(adapted from the radio play by
Ernest Dudley)

The elderly woman sighed, and twisted and turned in her bed. The little carriage clock on the small table at her bedside showed the hour of midnight. Yet alongside the clock, her telephone was ringing insistently.

The jangling noise finally penetrated her consciousness. Opening her eyes, she sat up and leaned across to the instrument. She picked up the receiver.

'Hello?' she whispered timorously.

'Is that you, Miss Nicholson?' the male voice on the line sounded slightly muffled.

'Yes, this is Miss Nicholson speaking. Who's that?'

'This is a friend,' said the voice on the telephone. 'Just to warn you to be on your guard.'

Miss Nicholson frowned worriedly. 'Be on my guard? What do you mean? Who are you?'

'I told you,' answered the strange voice, 'it's a friend . . . warning you. Someone's after your money, Miss Nicholson, so be on your guard.'

Miss Nicholson was now fully awake, and regaining something of her composure. 'Who are you?' she demanded sharply, and glanced at the clock. A slight chink in the curtains allowed a small shaft of illumination from the street light outside to show its face. 'And what do you mean waking me up at this hour?'

The man's tone hardened. 'Be on your guard. They know about your money you've got hidden away . . . '

'Oh!' A note of fear returned to her voice.

' . . . they'll go to any lengths to get it — even murder . . . '

At this Miss Nicholson almost dropped the telephone. 'What — ?' she gasped.

'Yes, Miss Nicholson — *Murder*!'

★ ★ ★

At her desk in Doctor Morelle's Harley Street office, Miss Frayle glanced up as she heard the ringing of the front door bell.

She frowned slightly. It was quite early in the morning, and the Doctor had no appointments for another hour or so.

'Who can that be at the door?' she thought to herself. 'Oh well, as Dr. Morelle would say, the best way to find out is to go and see.' She rose from her desk and moved to the doorway.

Crossing the small hallway, she opened the front door.

A small, elderly woman stood on the steps. She was dressed in good clothes that were somewhat worn. She was clutching the clasp of a large handbag.

Miss Frayle blinked in surprise behind her spectacles, then quickly recovered. 'Good morning,' she said politely.

'Oh, good morning,' the woman echoed. Then, anxiously, 'Is Doctor Morelle in?'

Miss Frayle instinctively became defensive. 'Oh — he's rather busy. He doesn't see anyone except by appointment.'

A faint look of alarm crossed the

woman's face. 'Oh . . . you see, it's rather urgent.'

Miss Frayle sighed involuntarily. 'Not another matter of life and death, I hope — ' she paused, slightly abashed that she had spoken her thoughts aloud.

The woman gave her an odd look. 'How funny you should say that. As it happens, it is.'

Miss Frayle gave a little start. 'Oh — oh, well — if it's as serious as that . . . Would you like to come in? I'll see if I can speak to the Doctor.'

'It's very kind of you,' the woman said, relieved, and stepped inside as Miss Frayle moved to the side of the doorway, opening the door wider.

Miss Frayle closed the front door and turned enquiringly to the woman as she stood in the hallway.

'My name is Miss Nicholson,' the woman said. 'Oh, I wouldn't trouble Doctor Morelle, only I know one of his patients. She spoke so very highly of him . . . and I'm most anxious to speak to him.'

'Oh, I'm so glad.' Miss Frayle took the

woman's elbow and guided her to the open doorway across the hall. She halted outside and regarded her with a slight trepidation, acutely aware of her employer's irascibility at unexpected callers. She asked firmly: 'Could you give me any idea what it's about Miss Nicholson?'

'Yes.' The woman fiddled with the clasp of her handbag, then looked up appealingly. 'You see — I'm going to be murdered.'

'I see . . . ' Miss Frayle responded automatically, then gave a start: 'Oh — did you say — *murdered*?'

'That's right.'

'Oh, yes — that's what I thought you said,' Miss Frayle became flustered. 'Oh dear, yes . . . well . . . '

'And I thought perhaps since you've been so kind,' the woman said with quiet dignity, 'Doctor Morelle might look into the matter.'

Miss Frayle recovered her composure and frowned. 'He's really most awfully busy.'

The woman nodded. 'Oh, I know I should have telephoned or written to ask him for an appointment.'

'It is usual.'

'But it might be too late by then,' the woman said.

'By when?'

'By tomorrow.'

Miss Frayle looked at the caller in astonishment. 'Oh . . . when do you expect to be murdered?'

'Oh, tonight.'

Inside his study, seated at his large desk, Doctor Morelle was dictating into a recording machine.

'When in the process of planning the crime, or in its actual perpetration, the criminal invariably fears the envy of the Gods. In the manner of the builders of the Temple of Nickle of Hondu in Japan, famous for its temples of the First and Third Shoguns of the Toligoi Dynasty. After the temple builders had created one sepulchre of flawless beauty, they — realised it might evoke the Gods' envy and so to appease them, they deliberately made a mistake in the symmetry in one of the columns . . . ' He broke off as there was a knocking at the door. He tightened his lips and looked towards the door as it opened slowly.

Miss Frayle came in, clenching her fingers nervously. 'Doctor, I'm so sorry to interrupt you . . . '

'You have finished your other work, Miss Frayle?' Doctor Morelle cut in.

'Yes, but . . . '

'Good, then perhaps I may continue dictating these notes to you instead of into this dictating machine.'

'Yes, doctor, but . . . '

'I would prefer that,' Doctor Morelle said decisively.

'Oh, would you?' Miss Frayle rallied: 'Well . . . there's a Miss Nicholson to see you.'

Doctor Morelle frowned. 'Who is she?'

Miss Frayle shrugged and spread her hands. 'Well, she's eccentric, I'm afraid. She's scared that she's going to be murdered. I did my best to get rid of her, but . . . '

Doctor Morelle alerted. 'Get rid of her, Miss Frayle?'

His secretary nodded unhappily. 'I — I know you don't like to be bothered with such stupid time-wasting cranks.'

Doctor Morelle smiled sardonically. 'You think that to see Miss Nicholson would be wasting my time?'

'Well, she did say something about one of your patients being a friend of hers, but — oh, she's obviously got some ridiculous bee in her bonnet.'

Doctor Morelle nodded. 'If that's your opinion, Miss Frayle . . . then, in that event . . . '

'It is most definitely,' Miss Frayle had recovered her confidence at what she thought was the Doctor's agreement at her assessment. 'I'll make some excuse. Don't worry.'

Dr. Morelle gave a thin smile. 'You interrupted me. I was about to say, well, in that event, it would be better if I *did* see her.'

'Oh!'

Doctor Morelle sat back in his chair. 'Will you please inform her that I'd be pleased to see her now.'

'Yes, Doctor,' Miss Frayle said faintly. 'I'll go and tell her.' She turned and hurried out.

* * *

Miss Nicholson had settled herself into the comfortable chair facing Dr. Morelle's desk. Miss Frayle had effected introductions, and then been dismissed to the adjoining office.

Preliminaries over, Doctor Morelle smiled at his visitor, and invited her to commence her story.

' . . . it started two weeks ago Doctor Morelle,' she was saying. 'Or is it a bit longer? Anyway, ever since that night, at twelve o'clock, someone has telephoned me warning me I'm in danger. That I'm going to be robbed of my money. And I heard mysterious footsteps outside the house when it's dark.'

Doctor Morelle looked at her thoughtfully. 'You say it's a man's voice on the phone?'

'Yes,' Miss Nicholson nodded emphatically, 'always the same. It sounded as if he was disguising his voice, but he was definitely a man.'

'Where do you live?' Doctor Morelle asked.

'Number 5 River Street, Chelsea. It's

just off the Embankment.'

Doctor Morelle made a note on a scratchpad. 'You live all alone?'

'Except for my dog.' Miss Nicholson smiled faintly. 'He's been with me eleven years — he's getting on a bit, but it's only a small house you see, and I can manage quite well for myself. My tastes are very simple.'

Doctor Morelle looked at the woman's clothing. It was of good quality, but worn. Then he asked: 'Have you any relations?'

'Not one, I'm afraid.' A fleeting sadness flickered across her face. 'There was my brother, but I haven't seen him for three years. He lives abroad. Last time I heard he was in . . . New Zealand, I think . . . Or was it South Africa?' she finished vaguely.

'And you have no idea who might want to cause you any harm?'

'None at all. I really can't think of anyone. Oh . . . ' the woman frowned as a thought struck her. 'Well, there was this — ah, but it couldn't be him.'

'Who, Miss Nicholson?' Doctor Morelle asked sharply.

'Well, it's only that my dog does bark at strange noises. One or two people have complained. There was Mr. er . . . oh, but no, it couldn't be him.'

Doctor Morelle changed the subject. 'Why didn't you deposit your money in the bank?' he asked briefly.

Miss Nicholson gave a little start. 'What money, doctor? I haven't got any money.'

'Then why should this anonymous well-wisher think you have?' Doctor Morelle pressed.

Miss Nicholson shrugged. 'Oh, I suppose it's some rumour that's got about because I live alone, or perhaps because I keep a dog. I don't know really.'

'Miss Nichsolson,' Doctor Morelle spoke deliberately, 'why have you come to me instead of going to the police?'

'Because this friend of mine who was a patient of yours, Miss Hanshaw — no, it wasn't her . . . Anyway, she said you were very clever.'

Doctor Morelle gave a thin smile. 'That was extremely kind of her.'

'Besides,' Miss Nicholson elaborated,

'the police don't believe me. They think I'm just a silly old woman.'

Doctor Morelle shook his head. 'I can't believe that.'

'It's true,' the woman insisted. 'I went to them when this horrid business first started. They just said they'd put someone on to keep a watch. I'm sure I haven't seen a policeman about.'

'You would be in your bed when he's on duty,' Doctor Morelle pointed out.

'I always take a look outside before I go to bed at night.'

'But it might be a plainclothes detective. You wouldn't realise it was a police officer.'

'Then surely they could catch this man who telephoned?' the woman said plaintively. 'I told them it's every night at the same time.'

'Well, it may present some difficulties,' Doctor Morelle demurred. 'Doubtless, he makes the calls from different places.'

'He did say something about that,' Miss Nicholson conceded. 'Anyway, they were full of excuses.'

Doctor Morelle rose, and smiled

gravely. 'However, leave the matter in my hands and I will do all in my power to ensure that a stop is put to the trouble.'

Miss Nicholson gave a little sigh of relief as she rose also. 'I knew you would help me.'

Doctor Morelle came round from behind his desk and stood looking down at Miss Nicholson as she straightened up. 'As to the threat to your life and property, I imagine you need not take that too seriously. It is hardly likely that anyone would take the trouble to warn you of their intentions. After all, forewarned is forearmed.'

'I suppose not. Thank you, Doctor Morelle, so much.'

He turned and pressed a button on his desk.

A moment later, responding to the buzzer, Miss Frayle entered.

'Yes, Doctor?'

'Miss Nicholson is just going, Miss Frayle.'

Miss Frayle smiled at the visitor and gently touched her elbow. 'Oh yes, Miss Nicholson. I'll see you to the door.'

'Thank you. And I'm most grateful to you, Doctor.'

'I'm sure we'll soon put your mind at rest,' he reassured her.

'Thank you so much. I can't say how really very grateful I am to you . . . '

'This way, Miss Nicholson.' Miss Frayle saw the elderly woman out and returned to Doctor Morelle's study, to find that he had resumed his seat behind the desk and was studying his notes.

'Well, Doctor, do you really think she's in danger of being murdered?' she asked curiously. Then she gave a start. 'What . . .?'

He looked up. 'What, Miss Frayle?'

Miss Frayle pointed to the chair where Miss Nicholson had been sitting. A handbag was on the floor at the side of the chair. 'Her handbag, she's left it behind.' She gave him an accusing look.

'I was under the impression that it was yours,' he said smoothly.

'Oh, really, Doctor Morelle! I wouldn't be seen dead with a thing like that.'

'I sincerely hope she won't,' he said dryly.

Miss Frayle bent to pick it up. 'Hmm,

it's more like an outsize tea cosy or something. Oh, poor thing. She won't have her bus fare home.'

'You'd better hurry after her.'

'Yes.' Miss Frayle snatched up the bag. 'Oh dear, the clasp's broken. Doctor Morelle . . . look . . . Five-pound notes — wads of them. Her bag's full of fivers!'

Doctor Morelle came round and looked into the bag in Miss Frayle's hands. 'It would appear to be quite a large sum.'

'Oh, and I was worrying about her bus fare. There must be a thousand pounds here. Oh well, she can't have got very far.' Miss Frayle closed the bag as best she could, and hurried to the doorway. Looking back, she added: 'I'll be right back, Doctor.'

'I do hope so.' Doctor Morelle gave a thin smile. 'All seaports, railway termini and airports will be watched.'

Miss Frayle hovered in the doorway. 'What do you mean?'

'In case you are harbouring an intention to flee the country with the loot, Miss Frayle.'

His secretary laughed. 'Oh, Dr. Morelle, really. You've quite made my heart turn over.'

A few moments later Miss Frayle was stepping out into the street. She glanced about her.

'She's nowhere in Harley Street. I'll just dash down to the corner.'

There wasn't any sign of Miss Nicholson. The woman had completely vanished.

'Oh well,' Miss Frayle thought to herself, 'she'll soon come dashing back when she realises she's left it behind. I'd better go back to Doctor Morelle.'

Within a couple of minutes she had returned to the study. 'No luck, Dr. Morelle — she's vanished into the blue.'

'Or probably into a taxi,' he commented. 'Now perhaps, I could proceed with dictating my notes.'

Anticipating this, Miss Frayle was already holding her notepad and pencil. She moved to her chair near the desk, and murmured: 'Well, I don't suppose it'll be long before she turns up again.'

Doctor Morelle ignored her comment. 'I had arrived at the elusion to the criminal's obsession that the Fates will envy his success and were citing the temple builders of old Japan. Now . . . where had I got to? Temple builders of . . . Let me switch on the machine.'

The Doctor's recorded voice sounded: 'After the temple builders had created one sepulchre of flawless beauty, they realised it might evoke the Gods' envy and so to appease them, they deliberately made a mistake in the symmetry in one of the columns . . . '

Doctor Morelle switched off the machine and nodded. 'That was it.'

'It's the same as the Persian rug-makers, isn't it?' Miss Frayle commented surprisingly. 'They leave a flaw in the design so that Allah won't think they're trying to create something completely perfect in his sight. That's the way you can tell a Persian rug if it's genuine.'

Doctor Morelle was singularly unimpressed. 'Might I be permitted to continue with what I was about to say?' he said coldly.

'Oh yes, doctor. I was only . . . '

'Thank you, Miss Frayle,' he said

heavily. Then he commenced dictating: 'The criminal believes that mere intelligence and cunning will provide him with protection against this vengeance of the Gods, and it is this factor which subconsciously urges him to commit some mistake in the crime he perpetrates which provides a clue for the investigative detective to follow up to the culprit's inevitable downfall . . . '

* * *

Later that day Miss Frayle picked up the ringing telephone.

'Hello. This is Doctor Morelle's house.'

'It's Miss Nicholson here,' the caller's voice said. 'I'm so sorry to bother you . . . it's my handbag . . . '

'Oh hello, Miss Nicholson. It's all right, your handbag is here, it's perfectly safe.'

'I must have left it behind . . . ' Miss Nicholson said vaguely.

'It's all right, Miss Nicholson, it's here,' Miss Frayle reassured her.

'Could you have a look — Oh, oh, you say it's there? You've found it?'

'Yes, I rushed after you with it, but you'd gone.'

'Oh, I happened to get a taxi as it was passing,' Miss Nicholson explained. 'I didn't realize I hadn't got it until I reached home. Do forgive me for giving you all this bother.'

'Oh, that's all right. By the way, the clasp came undone. There appears to be some money . . . '

'Oh, yes. What a nuisance . . . '

'It's quite safe. Only you ought to have it mended, you know.'

'Yes, yes, I know. It's always happening.'

'When will you come back for it?' Miss Frayle asked, endeavouring to bring the rambling conversation to an end.

'Well . . . ' Miss Nicholson said hesitantly, 'I simply must get lunch for my dog now. He's very old, you see, and it upsets his digestion if his meals aren't served regularly.'

'This afternoon then, I shall be in,' Miss Frayle said patiently.

'Well . . . I always rest in the afternoon. I was wondering if I could call tomorrow.'

'Yes, of course.'

'Though there are one or two things in it . . . ' Miss Nicholson began uncertainly.

'Such as a thousand pounds!' Miss Frayle muttered to herself.

' . . . such as my keys,' Miss Nicholson said.

'I was wondering how you got in,' Miss Frayle remarked.

'Oh, not my front door key. I always leave that under the mat. No, it's the keys to my desk. Oh dear, how silly of me.'

'I tell you what, Miss Nicholson,' Miss Frayle offered, 'I'll bring it along this evening.'

'Oh no, I can't put you to all that inconvenience.'

Miss Frayle smiled. 'Oh no, it isn't really. I'll be along about six.'

Relief tinged her caller's voice. 'Oh, you're most awfully kind. I'm very grateful.'

'No trouble at all. See you then.'

'Goodbye. I really must be going. Billy Boy will be famished.'

Miss Frayle wrinkled her brow. 'Who?'

'Goodbye, and thank you very much.'

As Miss Frayle put down the phone,

she suddenly realized that 'Billy Boy' must have been Miss Nicholson's dog. She turned to look at Doctor Morelle who had raised his eyebrows in mild enquiry. 'That was Miss Nicholson, Doctor. I'm going to return her handbag for her this evening.'

'She made no comment regarding the money?' he asked shrewdly.

'No, she didn't say anything.'

'I see.' Doctor Morelle reflected briefly, then: 'Would you get me Embankment Police Station on the phone, Miss Frayle?'

'Embankment Police Station? Yes, Doctor.'

'I would like to speak to the Superintendent, he may have some information on this matter.'

A few minutes later the Doctor was through to the Superintendent at the Embankment Police Station on the telephone.

' . . . I got the name and address, Doctor Morelle,' the Superintendent was saying. 'Miss Nicholson, No. 5 River Street, Chelsea. From what you're saying it's doubtful if she's been to the police about it all.'

'It has occurred to me, Superintendent, that as she'd been apparently less than truthful about the state of her finances, she might have lied concerning the other matter.'

'The fact of the phone calls still persisting suggests that she hasn't put in a complaint,' the Superintendent agreed. 'If she had, the Post Office would have been notified and arrangements made for the call to be intercepted by the exchange operator . . .'

'So that Miss Nicholson would be no longer troubled by them,' Doctor Morelle finished for him.

'That's the least that would have been done. Steps might even have been taken to try and nab the caller.'

'Precisely, Superintendent.'

'Yes . . . I expect she imagined the whole thing. Plenty of people going about believing something that's never really happened.'

'Nevertheless,' the Doctor said gravely, 'I've telephoned to confirm whether or not Miss Nicholson has been in touch with you.'

'Quite. You don't want to take any chances. Nor do we for that matter. I'll ring you back, Doctor. I'll give the station officer a buzz.'

The Superintendent was as good as his word, and shortly thereafter he was speaking to the Station Officer on the internal phone.

'Yes, sir,' that worthy answered. 'What's the name . . . ? A Miss Nicholson? Not here. No, no one of that name's made any complaint like that. If anything comes in, I'll let you know.'

He put down the receiver and coughed. 'Bit of a fog coming up from the river,' he murmured.

Not long afterwards, a tall, aesthetic-looking man presented himself at the Embankment Police Station, and regarded the Station Officer uncertainly. 'Good afternoon,' he ventured.

'Oh, I don't know what's good about it,' the policeman growled.

'Yes, it is a bit foggy,' the man agreed mildly.

'Fair hangs about your chest — ' the Station Officer broke off with a cough.

'You're the officer in charge? Er, I'm not very used to police stations . . . ' the man's voice trailed off. 'In fact, I've never been in one before.'

The policeman eyed him carefully, then decided to be more amiable. 'Always got to be a first time, sir. What can I do for you?'

'Well, I've called about something that I thought you might care to investigate.'

'Oh, yes,' the Station Office encouraged. 'And you are — ?'

'My name's Julian Smith. I'm an artist and I live in a small house in River Street.'

'River Street?' the policeman immediately alerted.

'It's quite near here.' The man misunderstood the response.

'Oh, I know, sir.' The policeman smiled encouragingly. 'Please continue.'

'My next door neighbour is an eccentric spinster named Nicholson. During the past week or more I've heard footsteps outside her house at night and several times I've heard her telephone ringing at midnight.'

The Station Officer's eyes narrowed. 'You work late I suppose, Mr. Smith?'

'Oh, often. Just now I'm rushing through some work.'

'What was it about these footsteps and phone ringing that made you think it ought to be reported?'

'Well . . . just that it sounded a bit mysterious, the phone going like that. It struck me as being a bit odd. Miss Nicholson lives alone and apart from being a funny old girl, she's rumoured to have a considerable amount of money tucked away in the old sock, or under the mattress.'

The Station Officer absorbed this information, then asked: 'Something else which aroused your suspicions?'

Smith shrugged. 'No — that's all, officer. I just thought I should let you know, in case . . . ' he paused uncertainly. 'I hope I haven't wasted your time.'

'On the contrary, Mr. Smith. We appreciate your coming here. I'll certainly see that it's enquired into.'

Smith nodded. 'Right. Good afternoon.'

'Good afternoon, sir. Thank you very

much.' As Smith went out, the officer smiled to himself and picked up the telephone.

'Put me through to the Superintendent, will you?'

★　★　★

A clock was chiming six, in Miss Nicholson's home. She glanced towards the bay window, and frowned. 'Dear me, it's so very dark with this horrid fog. I think I'll draw the curtains.' Rising from her armchair, she went to the windows, and closed the heavy drapes. Then she crossed to the far wall and switched on the electric light.

'There. That makes it cosier.' She glanced down at her pet dog as she returned to her chair. 'Lie still, Billy Boy. You stay warm by the fire, and you're not to bark when that young lady comes. She's bringing something for me. I hope she's not been delayed by the fog. It's so very kind of her to take all this trouble, and — '

She broke off as the telephone began

ringing. Immediately the dog began barking. The elderly woman glanced apprehensively towards the telephone, situated on a small table.

'Oh dear, I wish it wouldn't ring. It frightens me so.' The dog continued to bark as she hesitated. 'Be quiet Billy Boy. Oh, I don't know whether to answer it or not. Billy Boy — *be quiet*!'

The dog responded to her sharp tone, and fell silent.

'That's better. It must be the young woman to say she's been held up by the fog. I'd better answer it.'

Getting up she went to the telephone. As she did so, the dog started barking again. She turned: '*Be quiet*, Billy Boy!' She picked up the receiver. 'Hello?'

'Is this the number for Miss Nicholson?' asked a man's voice on the other end of the line.

'Miss Nicholson speaking. Who is that? *Be quiet*, Billy Boy. There's a good dog now.'

'This is Embankment Police Station. Station Officer speaking,' the caller's voice said.

'Oh.' Miss Nicholson gave a little start. 'Oh yes.'

'I thought I'd let you know that Doctor Morelle will be coming to see you this evening.'

'Oh — Oh yes, how very kind of him.'

'Superintendent Denham will be with him. They want to have a word with you, just to see that you're safe and secure.'

Miss Nicholson sat down slowly on a padded stool near the telephone table, still holding the receiver on its extended cord. 'Oh, how very kind.'

'It might have startled you, people arriving unexpectedly out of the fog,' the Station Officer explained. 'So I thought I'd let you know so you won't be scared when they come.'

'How very thoughtful of you. So very kind. Oh . . . ' she paused as she heard sounds from outside. 'I think I can hear someone now. No — no, it can't be. Billy Boy would have barked.'

'Well, they wouldn't have arrived yet.' There was a note of puzzlement in the caller's voice.

'Yet I thought I heard footsteps

outside . . . ' Miss Nicholson faltered, then she smiled. 'Ah yes, it'll be the young woman I'm expecting from Doctor Morelle. Will you hold on please while I go and see? I don't want to leave her outside in that fog.'

She put the receiver down carefully, and crossed to the living room door, which opened onto a small hallway, at the end of which was the front door.

Popping her head into the hallway she called out: 'I'm just coming.' She glanced behind her as the dog scrambled up from the floor and made to follow her out of the room.

'No, Billy Boy. You wait there. You don't want to go out in that nasty fog.' Reaching the front door, she opened it. 'Is that you Miss . . . Oh — who is it? Oh . . . *oooooooh!*'

★ ★ ★

The fog was quite thick in the street near the embankment. A taxi, headlights blazing, slowed to a stop.

The taxi driver twisted round to

address his passenger in the back of the cab. 'We're in River Street all right, Miss. Know which end it is?'

'I'm afraid not,' Miss Frayle answered.

The taxi driver wound down his nearside window, and leaned outside. 'Fog's not getting no better.' He gave a chesty cough.

Miss Frayle blinked behind her thick spectacles. 'What's the number we've stopped at?'

'I'm trying to see, Miss . . . Looks like 29 — yes, 29. Opposite side is 30. So number 5 must be the other end of the street.'

'Yes,' Miss Frayle agreed.

'Got our bearings a bit, anyway,' the driver commented. 'I'll drive slow. We don't want to end up in the river, do we?'

'No, we don't really.' Miss Frayle fell silent as the driver restarted the taxi, and edged slowly along the roadside.

At length the taxi neared the end of the street. 'Here we are, number 5 it is.' The taxi driver switched off the engine, and got out. He opened the passenger door.

'Thank you,' Miss Frayle said, as she

slid out carefully, clutching Miss Nicholson's handbag. 'You've been awfully clever to find the house in this fog.'

'That's all right, Miss.' The driver closed the door behind her.

'Would you wait for me, please? I — I shan't be a few minutes.'

'All right, Miss,' the driver assented. 'Mind how you go. You can't see yer 'and before yer.'

Miss Frayle smiled faintly. 'I don't really want to see a hand before me.'

She stepped across the pavement and peered myopically at the doorway of No. 5. She discerned a bell-push just below the letterbox and pressed it firmly.

The door swung gently inwards.

'Oh, the door's half open.'

The door creaked slightly as Miss Frayle pushed it further open. 'Miss Nicholson — are you there?' she called. No answer. She raised her voice: 'Miss Nicholson . . . It's Miss Frayle from Doctor Morelle.'

Complete silence greeted her.

'No one at home — not even her dog,' Miss Frayle murmured, closing the front door behind her, to cut off the swirls of fog trying to creep inside. But she did not close it entirely. 'Perhaps she's fallen asleep.' She advanced along the short hall and reached the open living room door, from which light was spilling into the passage. She glanced inside and around the room. It was empty.

Miss Frayle stepped back and noticed a closed door on the opposite side of the narrow hall. 'I'll try in there.'

She opened the door to the sitting room with one hand, Miss Nicholson's mislaid handbag tightly held in the other. It was somewhat gloomy, the only direct illumination coming from the fog-shrouded window. Miss Frayle pushed the door wide, to allow the light from the opposite room to spill into it.

She saw the huddled figure clearly.

Miss Frayle put a hand to her mouth in horror. 'Oh, Miss Nicholson . . . oh, she's — *she's dead*! I just know she is!' Oh, I must get help. 'Where's the phone . . . ' Miss Frayle turned nervously at the sound of footsteps in the hall. 'Who's there . . . who is it?'

'Are you all right, Miss?'

Miss Frayle let out a relieved sigh at the sound of a familiar voice. 'Oh, oh, it's you driver.'

'I wondered what had happened.' He caught sight of the pathetic figure of Miss Nicholson lying on the carpet. 'Blimey, is she . . . '

'I think she's dead, Miss Frayle whispered.'

The driver stepped forward. 'Want me to help you lift her?'

'Oh, no.' Miss Frayle laid a restraining hand on his shoulder. 'I don't think we ought to touch her.'

'Why?' the driver looked his puzzlement. 'What do you mean?'

Suddenly there was the sound of whimpering.

'What's that?' Miss Frayle faltered.

'It's a dog,' the driver said, looking at the cowed animal, which had evidently followed him in from the street.

'Oh, Miss Nicholson's dog. He must have dashed out when the door was left open.' Miss Frayle looked at the whimpering dog, and added pityingly: 'He knows something's happened.'

'We'd better get him into the next room,' the driver observed.

'Yes, come on.' Miss Frayle was anxious to get away from the body. 'The phone'll be in there. Oh, I must get Doctor Morelle.'

The dog resumed barking, and Miss Frayle and the driver turned at the sound of a deep voice.

'What's going on?'

'A copper!' the driver exclaimed.

'The police,' Miss Frayle corrected.

'That's right,' the officer said heavily. 'I'm from Embankment Police Station.' He came forward and looked between them into the room beyond. He caught sight of the huddled body. 'Who's this?' he asked sharply.

'Miss Nicholson,' Miss Frayle told him, adding in a whisper: 'I found her.'

'So this is Miss Nicholson, eh? And you found her like this?'

'Yes.'

'Let's have a look at her.' The policeman entered the room and dropped to one knee. After a few moments he straightened up, grim-faced.

'Is she — is she dead?' Miss Frayle asked timorously.

'Seems like it,' the officer said briefly.

'Oh, poor thing.'

The officer began to assert his authority. He looked at Miss Frayle. 'Perhaps we might know who you are, Miss.'

'Well, I'm Miss Frayle. Doctor Morelle's secretary.'

'Doctor Morelle?' the officer's eyebrows rose.

'Yes. I came here by taxi from Harley Street.'

'That's right,' the driver confirmed gallantly. 'I brought her here.'

The officer looked at him. 'That your cab outside?'

'That's right,' the man nodded vigorously.

The policeman looked at Miss Frayle again. 'And what would you be doing here?'

'This handbag,' Miss Frayle lifted the bag she had been clutching tightly. 'She left it behind when she called to see Doctor Morelle this afternoon.'

'So you were returning it?' The officer extended a hand. 'May I have a look please.'

'There's a lot of money in it,' Miss

Frayle said. 'The clasp has broken.'

'Hmm. It's full of five pound notes.' Suspicion tinged the policeman's voice. 'And you say you're Miss Frayle?'

'Well of course!' Miss Frayle gave him an indignant look. 'Surely you don't think I had anything to do with this?'

''Course she didn't,' the driver said supportively. 'I can swear to that.'

'Oh, I believe you, Miss.' The officer softened his voice. 'But this is a bit of an odd business.'

Miss Frayle recovered herself a little, and said briskly: 'You can easily phone Doctor Morelle. He'll confirm who I am and what I came here for.'

'No need for that,' the policeman said surprisingly. 'Doctor Morelle's already on his way here.'

Miss Frayle was startled at this news. 'Oh — but — I mean, how can he know what happened?'

'He must be psychic!' the driver commented dryly.

The policeman smiled and shook his head. 'He isn't. Superintendent Denham's bringing him. They wanted to have a chat with her. Something fishy's going on and the Superintendent spoke with Doctor Morelle.'

Miss Frayle gave a start. 'I've just remembered something! Miss Nicholson . . . she said she was going to be murdered tonight!'

The dog started barking again.

'That'll be them now,' the policeman said.

Miss Frayle bent and patted the dog's head. 'Quiet. It's all right now. Be quiet.'

The small party moved in the hall passageway.

'Is that you, Superintendent?' the Station Officer called, looking towards the door as it swung open.

'Yes,' the Superintendent's voice answered him.

'Oh, Doctor Morelle will be with him,' Miss Frayle commented thankfully.

The taxi driver looked at the policeman. 'I'd better get back to my taxi in case anything's happened to it.' The officer gave him an approving nod.

Miss Frayle called out as the familiar, tall saturnine figure of the Doctor appeared behind Superintendent Denham.

'Doctor Morelle, it's me, Miss Frayle,' she gushed.

'So I perceive,' was the dry response.

The Station Officer lost no time in bringing his superior up to speed. 'And it was while you went out, Superintendent, I was on the phone to Miss Nicholson about you and Doctor Morelle looking in on her, when she asked me to hold on. Someone was at the door, she said. And as she didn't come back to the phone, I thought something had happened. So I came round here quick as I could.'

'And Miss Nicholson?' Superintendent Denham asked sharply.

'Miss Frayle had got here before me. She found her.'

Doctor Morelle flashed a look at his secretary. 'Where is Miss Nicholson?' he rapped.

Miss Frayle indicated the side door of the sitting room. 'In here, doctor. She's . . .'

'She's had it, I'm afraid,' the policeman said heavily.

The Superintendent gave him a keen glance. 'You didn't hear who it was who came in while you were on the phone?'

The Officer shrugged. 'Not a thing.'

'You wait there, Miss Frayle,' Doctor Morelle instructed, moving towards the door and grasping the handle.

'Yes, doctor,' she whispered.

'Just go in, Doctor Morelle,' the Superintendent said, as the Doctor paused, his hand on the door. 'I'll follow you.' He glanced at the Station Officer. 'Better call an ambulance,' he instructed.

'There's a phone in the living room opposite,' Miss Frayle said.

'I'll do that, Superintendent,' the policeman said, crossing the hall.

'And tell them at the Yard,' the Superintendent called after him, 'watch out for fingerprints.'

The policeman entered the living room, Miss Frayle hovering uncertainly behind him. He looked at the telephone. 'Whoever it was put the receiver back. Be some delay getting here in this fog . . . '

In the room opposite, Superintendent Denham regarded the pathetic figure of Miss Nicholson as Doctor Morelle bent to examine her. 'What's it look like to you, Doctor Morelle?'

Straightening up, Doctor Morelle appeared to be slipping something into his pocket. 'Obviously attacked by someone with a heavy stick, or something similar,' he said.

'Yes . . . it looks as if she was dragged into this side room out of the way.'

Doctor Morelle glanced around the neat room. 'Nothing seems to have been disturbed.'

'Well, whoever it was must have been scared off,' the Superintendent decided. 'Maybe the dog. Let's go back to the others.'

As they entered the sitting room, the Station Officer turned from the telephone table, carefully replacing the handkerchief he had used whilst phoning. 'Ambulance is on its way, Superintendent. The Yard told me that the fog outside is getting thicker than ever. But they're on their way.'

Doctor Morelle glanced at Superintendent Denham. 'May I question your officer, Superintendent?'

'Surely — go right ahead. I've a few things to ask him myself, as well.'

Doctor Morelle turned to the Station Officer. 'When you were on the phone and Miss Nicholson asked you to hold on while she went to answer the door, you heard nothing?'

'Not exactly, sir. I heard her put down the receiver and I heard her call out to someone.'

'You didn't hear anyone else's voice?' Denham asked sharply.

'No . . . ' the policeman reflected, then: 'Oh, come to think of it, Superintendent. Mightn't this fit in with that artist chap . . . '

'Who came to see you this afternoon?' Denham supplied, his eyes narrowing.

'Called himself Julian Smith,' the policeman said, his tone tinged with scepticism.

'Are you suggesting it is he who was telephoning at night and prowling around the house?' Doctor Morelle asked.

The Superintendent nodded, a definite hypothesis building up in his mind. 'And then he calls at the police station to build up an alibi.'

Miss Frayle had been listening respectfully without speaking, as ever half afraid that anything she said would be dismissed by the Doctor. But at the Superintendent's words she couldn't help express her puzzlement.

'But why should he do that?'

Denham looked at her, and spread his hands: 'He lives next door. He'd want to point the finger of suspicion away from himself.' He turned to the Doctor. 'What do you think, Doctor Morelle?'

'It is a possibility,' he conceded.

'Yes . . . ' the Superintendent sighed. 'If only she hadn't lied to you the way she did.'

'You mean about not having any money?' Miss Frayle asked, now feeling emboldened enough to contribute further to the discussion.

Denham nodded. 'Yes, and that she'd been to the police when she hadn't. We could have prevented all this.'

At that moment the dog began barking again.

'Be quiet,' Miss Frayle said.

'Sounds like someone at the door,' Denham said.

A man's voice called out: 'Who's there? Is anyone there? Miss Nicholson . . . ?'

'It's that man Smith,' the Station Officer said, immediately recognizing the voice.

The Superintendent exchanged a look with Doctor Morelle. 'Returning to the scene of his crime, eh, Dr. Morelle?'

All eyes turned to Smith as he reached the living room door and edged into the room. 'Anyone at home? Miss Nicholson, you all right — I saw your door open . . . oh!' he broke off in confusion as he saw the assembly.

'Good evening, Mr. Smith,' the policeman said heavily.

'Oh, it's you officer,' Smith said, looking uncertainly at the others.

'And this is Superintendent Denham . . . ' the officer introduced, ' . . . Mr. Julian Smith.'

'And Doctor Morelle. Not forgetting Miss Frayle,' Denham added.

Smith was recovering his poise. 'Oh, quite a party. What's happened to Miss Nicholson?'

'You wouldn't have any idea about that?' Denham snapped.

Smith appeared surprised. 'No. Why

should I?' As the Superintendent remained silent and uncompromising, he added defensively: 'I was a bit concerned about her welfare. That's why I called at the police station yesterday, as this officer will tell you.'

'You say you noticed the front door open?' Doctor Morelle asked him smoothly.

'I was passing on my way home,' Smith answered. 'I saw the taxi cab waiting and then the door open. I had a feeling something was wrong. I'm sensitive to that sort of thing.'

'No doubt you would be,' Doctor Morelle said dryly.

'Artistic temperament and all that,' Smith explained. 'And so I came in.'

The dog started barking again.

'What's he barking for this time?' Miss Frayle frowned. Then she brightened: 'Oh, it may be the ambulance.'

'I'll go and give them a hand,' the policeman volunteered, and went to the door.

'And I would like to have a word with the attendants,' Doctor Morelle murmured, following him.

'Shall I come too, doctor?' Miss Frayle asked.

Doctor Morelle gave her a thin smile and shook his head. 'There is nothing you can do, Miss Frayle.'

The Superintendent resumed his questioning. 'Mr. Smith, you told the Station Officer about hearing the telephone ringing here at night and footsteps.'

Smith nodded, 'I work late in my studio and I've been hearing the phone ring at midnight and then these footsteps, as if someone was creeping about the place.'

'You heard this last night?'

'Yes. That's what made me go to the police station. I thought it was about time it should be reported.'

'Hmmm,' Denham murmured, unconvinced. 'Very public spirited of you.'

'I was afraid the old girl might have been in some danger,' Smith said. 'And it looks as if I was right, too.'

'It certainly does, Mr. Smith,' Denham agreed dryly, then turned as Doctor Morelle and the policeman re-entered the room.

'The ambulance is just going,' the Doctor reported.

'Still no sign of the Yard, sir,' the officer said worriedly. 'The fog must be holding them up,'

'Oh, they'll be here,' Denham said confidently. Then he noticed Doctor Morelle taking a small object from his pocket. 'Something significant, Doctor?'

'Only this.' Doctor Morelle opened his palm.

'What is it?' Miss Frayle asked excitedly.

'Book of matches,' Denham said, taking the small box as Doctor Morelle extended his hand towards him.

'Found underneath the body,' Doctor Morelle said levelly.

The Superintendent narrowed his eyes and glanced about him. 'Well, since this house appears to be all electric . . . '

'Are you aware, Mr. Smith,' Doctor Morelle asked him, 'whether or not Miss Nicholson smoked?'

Smith shook his head. 'I didn't see her often, but I don't remember noticing that she did smoke, and . . . ' he broke off as a middle-aged man suddenly entered the room.

Doctor Morelle glanced at the dog, which remained silent. He smiled thinly.

'What's happened?' the newcomer asked.

'And who are you?' Denham demanded in return.

The man frowned. 'Is anything wrong? My name's Nicholson. I'm Miss Nicholson's brother.'

Miss Frayle assumed a sympathetic expression. 'I'm afraid that . . . ' she began.

'Something's happened to her,' Nicholson blurted. 'I saw the ambulance outside.'

'Take it easy, Mr. Nicholson,' the Superintendent said firmly. 'I'm Superintendent Denham of Embankment Police Station . . . and this is Dr. Morelle and . . . '

'She's dead,' Nicholson cut in. 'This is terrible!'

'I knew Miss Nicholson slightly,' Doctor Morelle stepped forward. 'She said something about having a brother in New Zealand or South Africa . . . '

'South Africa,' Nicholson supplied.

189

'I only got back a couple of days ago. I haven't seen her since three years.'

Doctor Morelle regarded him thoughtfully. 'So she wasn't expecting you?'

Nicholson shook his head vigorously. 'No, nothing like that.' He glanced at the two officers and frowned. 'But should the police be here?'

'I'm afraid your sister was attacked by someone,' Denham informed him.

'Murdered you mean?' Nicholson looked dismayed. 'But who'd want to murder her?'

'That's what we're here to find out.' Denham said grimly.

Smith was looking slightly uneasy. 'I think I might as well be getting along,' he murmured.

Denham swung to him. 'If you wouldn't mind waiting, Mr. Smith. There's just one or two questions I'd like to ask you.'

'Well, I'd . . . '

'Unless you're in a very great hurry to leave?' Denham demanded.

Smith shrugged resignedly. 'Oh, no, no, that's all right.'

'Thank you, Mr. Smith,' Denham said.

190

'You see — ' he broke off in surprise as the telephone began ringing.

Miss Frayle instinctively moved to answer it. 'Hello. Yes . . . It's for you, Doctor Morelle.'

Doctor Morelle was already moving towards her. He took the receiver as she handed it to him. 'Doctor Morelle here . . . ' he paused, listening. 'Good. Thank you.' He turned and smiled thinly at Nicholson. 'That was the hospital, Mr. Nicholson. You may be glad to learn that there is every hope that your sister will recover.'

Miss Frayle goggled. 'She wasn't dead after all?'

A peculiar expression settled on Nicholson's face. 'Not dead? She's . . . she's alive?'

'It was a near thing,' Doctor Morelle commented. His voice hardened: 'But you didn't quite succeed in your attempt to murder her.'

'What?' Miss Frayle's jaw dropped.

Nicholson began to bluster. 'If you're trying to be funny, I don't think this is the time for it!'

A light dawned in Miss Frayle's mind. 'Doctor Morelle!' she exclaimed. 'The book of matches — '

The Superintendent's expression also changed. 'That's it, that's what brought you back after you left her for dead,' he challenged.

'I tell you . . . ' Nicholson continued to protest.

'You were afraid it would give you away,' Denham went on relentlessly.

Nicholson rallied. 'Well, you must be mad. I tell you I haven't seen my sister for three years. I've only just got back to London . . . '

'And where are you staying, Mr. Nicholson?' Doctor Morelle asked silkily.

'What's the name of your hotel?' Denham demanded harshly.

'My hotel?' Nicholson faltered.

'Shall I tell you?' Denham continued relentlessly. 'The Hotel Regal.' He held up the box he had taken from Doctor Morelle. 'Where these matches came from!'

Nicholson's bluster was replaced by panic. Suddenly he twirled and darted towards the doorway.

Before he could reach it, heavy footsteps sounded in the hallway and the dog began barking.

'I shouldn't try to run for it,' Denham called out after him.

'That'll be Scotland Yard,' the policeman said. 'Nice timing!'

* * *

Back at Doctor Morelle's residence, Miss Frayle wriggled comfortably in her chair. Doctor Morelle, seated at his desk, regarded her benignly.

'Well,' she remarked brightly, 'there's one thing about going out on a bleak and foggy night like this, Doctor. It's really nice to get back to Harley Street.'

'Yes, I'm anxious to continue work on those notes I had to leave.'

'I must say,' Miss Frayle said, 'I thought Superintendent Denham was jolly quick talking about those matches.'

'He was a trifle premature in fact,' Doctor Morelle commented, adding: 'Although, with justification.'

'One thing still puzzles me,' Miss Frayle said.

'Only one?' Doctor Morelle's tone was gently sarcastic.

'Why didn't you tell everyone that Miss Nicholson actually wasn't dead? You examined her, and said nothing to us!'

'Miss Nicholson was deeply unconscious, and I detected only the faintest of pulses — which evidently fooled the policeman when he made his cursory examination.' Doctor Morelle shrugged. 'To have attempted to awaken and question her would have been distinctly dangerous. I knew an ambulance was to be sent for, so I saw no point in discussing the matter . . . And now my dear Miss Frayle, perhaps — '

'Doctor, I've just thought of something!'

'Have you, Miss Frayle?' Doctor Morelle permitted himself a thin smile as he reached for an inevitable Le Sphinx cigarette from the skull on his desk.

'It wasn't really the matches after all!' she exclaimed triumphantly.

Doctor Morelle raised an eyebrow. 'No?'

'It was the dog.'

'You begin to interest me,' Doctor Morelle lit his cigarette and sat back.

'The barking dog, which barked at everyone who was a stranger, but not at the brother,' Miss Frayle smiled. 'That's it. Yes. I recollect now that the policeman didn't hear the dog over the phone when Miss Nicholson went to answer the door.'

Doctor Morelle said impatiently: 'If I may be permitted to begin dictating . . . '

'That was really what gave him away, wasn't it, doctor?' Miss Frayle insisted.

'Precisely, my dear Miss Frayle.'

'And you were keeping it up your sleeve!'

'I'm waiting, Miss Frayle,' Doctor Morelle said ominously.

'But, Doctor Morelle, doesn't the idea thrill you? That blessed dog, barking at all the innocent people and not at the one who was guilty. I mean, that's a classic example of . . . '

'It is in fact, my dear Miss Frayle,' Doctor Morelle interrupted, 'a classic example of that subconscious compulsion, that obsessive inner force, which urges the criminal to return to the scene of his crime.'

Miss Frayle laughed. 'Oh . . . oh . . . I was going to say, of a dog barking up the wrong tree.'

6

The Case of the Man Who Loved Clocks

Doctor Morelle neatly sorted the papers on his desk and pushed them aside. The scene was his quiet and shadowed study lit by the solitary desk lamp. The hour was late and the night was midsummer. He was just congratulating himself on being undisturbed by any outside influences — he had even remarked to that effect to Miss Frayle — when the telephone rang. He answered it himself.

'What is it?' he snapped irritably.

'Are you the Doctor?' came a perky Cockney voice over the wire.

'I am Doctor Morelle.'

'Well, listen.' There was a brief pause, then the man gulped out close to the mouthpiece: 'Old Woodham's bumped hisself orf!'

'Woodham?'

'Yerce! You know him. Used to come up West to mend your clocks.' The man's tone rose in pitch. 'Cor, you must remember him — little deaf and dumb watchmaker in Cleft Street, orf West India Dock Road.'

'Ah, yes, I recollect the man,' the Doctor murmured. 'Do I understand you to say he's committed *felo de se*?'

'Nah. He wouldn't do a thing like that. But he's gorn and bumped hisself orf, that's wot. I was passing his shop jest now, sees the door ajar, goes in and there he is. Pore blighter — ' The voice broke off for a second. Then it went on again irrepressibly. 'I knew he did some work for you, Doc, so I thought I'd better give you a tinkle.'

'What is your name?'

'Ah, that I ain't saying!' the man retorted with a mixture of defiance and intrigue. 'Catch me having the perlice pinching me for it!'

'But you've just stated it is suicide.'

'That's wot it looks like, but me and the cops ain't very friendly. Had one or two argyments, so I'm keeping mum. See!' In a more friendly tone the man went on: 'I was a pal of old Woodham's, or I wouldn't be tipping you orf like I am — '

'Now, just a minute, if you have information which may elucidate — '

'Well, I ain't telling you anything else, see! So long, Doc!' There was a metallic click at the other end of the telephone.

Doctor Morelle removed the receiver from his ear, eyed it distastefully, and drumming his other hand on the desk, replaced it in its cradle.

Miss Frayle paused in refilling the human skull that served as a container for the Doctor's Le Sphinx cigarettes.

'Is anything wrong, Doctor?' she asked anxiously. He ceased drumming his fingers and surveyed her contemplatively.

'Some anonymous informant has advised me of the deaf mute watchmaker, Woodham's demise,' he remarked impassively.

'The poor little man's dead?' her eyes widened. 'Oh, but that's terrible.'

'Apparently he committed suicide.'

'Suicide?'

'According to the person at the other end of the telephone who preferred to shroud his identity in anonymity.'

She goggled and fiddled with her spectacles.

'You mean he wouldn't give his name?'

'Precisely, my dear Miss Frayle.'

'What made him telephone, I wonder?'

He walked over to the skull, picked out a cigarette, tapped it, then noticing he already had a half-burnt cigarette, on a tray on his desk, replaced it casually.

'The man who telephoned,' he explained, 'claimed acquaintance with the deceased, and was aware that he did work for me upon occasion.' He picked up his gold cigarette case and strode to the door as though he had suddenly made a decision. 'But come, Miss Frayle. Bestir yourself from your unbecomingly lethargic posture.'

'Where are we going, Doctor?'

'To Limehouse.'

'L-L-Limehouse! At this time of night?'

'That is what I said.' He eyed her irritably. 'A hard-working and worthy quarter of London, much maligned in fiction, I fear. No doubt it is from that source you have gained your prejudice of the district . . .'

'But why should we go there tonight?'

'My dear Miss Frayle,' he said with a thin smile, 'must I again remind you that you are employed in the capacity of assistant and not as interrogator?'

She sighed and walked on to the landing. 'Well, if we must go, I'd better get your swordstick, Doctor.'

'Then hurry!' he called after her exasperatedly. 'It really is imperative that we proceed to Woodham's horological establishment in Cleft Street without delay.'

Half an hour later, Doctor Morelle was parking his car in West India Dock Road. They alighted and walked a few paces to Cleft Street, which they discovered to be a little back street within London's backwater of dockland where Asiatic wanderers of the world have found a resting place. Cleft Street, narrow and tortuous, sloped down to the Thames and the docks. Houses, stores, and shops tumbled against one another in huddled friendliness. A tug's siren hooted mournfully across the dark river. A door opened and they heard the tinkling music of an electric piano. Eerie shadows seemed to lurk in every doorway.

'By rights it ought to be foggy,' Miss Frayle commented with a shiver that was not invoked by the weather. 'But I'm glad it isn't!'

'Hm . . . fortuitously there is a moon, and it is not unduly cold for an English midsummer night,' the Doctor mused.

They peered at the names on the shop fronts. There was a Chinese laundry, a junk shop; an Indian Seamen's Club; and then a shop bearing the name, 'Samuel Woodham'. A dark blue paper blind was drawn down over the window.

Doctor Morelle halted and pushed at the door where the blistered paint was peeling crisply.

'This is the shop,' he observed. 'The door is slightly open. Let us enter.'

Miss Frayle shuddered as the door squeaked. She followed him reluctantly.

'Oh dear!' she flustered. 'I wish you didn't always drag me into your horrid cases!'

'Cease whining, Miss Frayle! Really, I do find you most exasperating.' He shone his torch round the shop.

'Observe! Woodham, it would appear,

was quite a connoisseur in bizarre horology.'

They saw scores of clocks of every description. Hideous presentation clocks in oak cases; grandfather clocks; china clocks, rococo in ornamentation; ingenious clocks worked by sand by dripping water; and even trick clocks camouflaged as frying pans, pictures and inkwells. The concerted ticking of these instruments, for the moment, had an almost soothingly mesmeric effect on Miss Frayle.

'Doubtless Woodham will be in the room at the back,' Doctor Morelle deduced, and manoeuvred his way through the overcrowded shop.

'Listen to all these clocks ticking!' Miss Frayle whispered in awed tones. 'Oh, it's so creepy. If only it wasn't so dark — Oh!' She started. 'What's that?'

A clock made a portentous whirring sound preparatory to striking three sombre chimes.

'Merely an extremely inaccurate timepiece!' he diagnosed calmly. 'This way, follow my torch. Doubtless we will ascertain the whereabouts of a light switch presently.'

He skirted the counter and observed a door on his left. He opened it, and felt inside for the switch. Miss Frayle drew back with a terror-stricken gasp as she peered into the illuminated workroom. On a long, scrubbed table there were parts of watches and tools. At one end was the head of a man with staring eyes, his chin resting horribly on the table. Doctor Morelle walked over quickly, discovering the man's huddled body propped on a low stool below the table.

Horror-stricken, she watched him examine a wound that gaped red on the man's right temple.

'Shot through the head,' he pronounced. 'Apparently a revolver of small calibre.' He glanced round and on the cracked linoleum-covered floor saw the shining butt of a revolver. 'This would be the weapon.' He bent down to inspect it.

'Is — is he quite dead?'

The Doctor snapped querulously: 'Really, Miss Frayle, your laxity of verbal expression is most reprehensible. A man is either dead — or he is not. He cannot be quite dead.'

'Oh — yes — I see. I — ' Her words ended in a little moan.

The Doctor jerked himself upright and saw her slim form swaying, her eyes strangely glassy. She clutched at a grandfather clock for support, and it seemed as though she would bring it crashing on top of her at any moment.

'Do pull yourself together and stand up!' he commanded raspingly. 'And kindly replace that timepiece in its appropriate position.'

'I'm — so — faint.'

With deliberate callousness he turned his back on her and reverted again to his investigation. Near to the dead man's right hand he observed an ordinary slate, as is often used by school children. Some words were scrawled on it.

'Hm . . . a communication anent Woodham's decease.' He held the slate to the light, and read slowly. ''I do not want to go on no moor . . . Everythink is too depressing and my head won't stand it . . . Tell my nefew Johnny I am sorry I dun it, but it's the best way. Yore's in dispare, S. Woodham'.'

He pondered for a moment. Then he commented: 'Extraordinary how such a first-class craftsman could be so illiterate. Do you not think so, Miss Frayle — ?'

She did not answer, and he looked up to see her unsteadily moving towards him, clinging to the table, her eyes alight with irrepressible indignation.

'I think — think you are very callous, Doctor,' she accused him. 'You saw me about to faint, and yet you turned your back on me! You'd have — have let me crash to the floor, bang my head and probably kill myself. But I wouldn't — wouldn't — let you have that satisfaction. I refused to faint!'

'Precisely,' he murmured with a supercilious smile. 'That is exactly what I anticipated. It was impossible for me to traverse the distance and catch you, therefore I had to resort to other measures to save you. By ignoring your malaise, I succeeded in curing it.'

'You really mean that was your intention, Doctor?' she stammered. 'You were anxious?'

'Most!' He turned from her abruptly,

snapping: 'It would have been signally inconvenient for me to have coped with two bodies!' He pushed the slate in front of her eyes. 'May I have your — er — valued opinion on this epistle?'

She read dazedly. 'You mean spelling nephew 'nefew' and 'yore's in dispare,' — 'yore's' and 'dispare'?'

He smiled almost cordially. 'I am pleased to observe you are recovering from your fainting spell sufficiently to note those errors.'

She said weakly: 'I do feel a little better — ' She broke off as she heard an oddly repetitive bird-like noise. 'Oh, what's that?'

'Merely a mechanical rendition of the species *Cuculus canorus*,' he said blandly.

'A cuckoo clock!'

'Precisely!'

'Oh, I feel shaky again, Doctor.'

He turned away from her and snapped: 'Sit down there and place your head between your knees.'

She did as he requested, staring at the faded check pattern of the linoleum.

'Why anyone with a fraction of

commonsense should be intimidated by what are easily explained phenomena I fail to comprehend,' he snapped. The cuckoo clock chirped again twice. 'What, for example, is startling about that?' the Doctor wanted to know. 'The contraption is obviously out of order, and there is little else to be said of it.'

From her crouching position Miss Frayle mumbled: 'I keep thinking about poor Mr. Woodham. What a shocking end for him! People have to feel right in the depths of melancholia before they can kill themselves. I know!' Shuddering, she thought of the nightmare occasion when she had been destitute and frenzied, and Doctor Morelle, encountering her for the first time, had prevented her from throwing herself into the Thames. The recollection that she had ever attempted suicide now filled her with shame and remorse. She said strangely reflectively: 'Suicide is the consummate act of self-pity, you know, Doctor.'

'Yes, yes, Miss Frayle,' he nodded abstractedly. 'However, people with disabilities such as a deaf-mute, are seldom self-commiserating. They possess greater moral courage than most of us.'

'Then why did he kill himself?' Her tone was raised with feeling.

'On the contrary, he did no such thing!'

'Doctor — you don't mean he was — ?' She dreaded to say the word.

He nodded grimly.

'Then — who did it?'

'Frankly, I do not know.'

'Well, how — how do you know it's murder? Are you quite sure?'

'My deduction is conclusively accurate — as always.' He waved a silencing hand. 'No, Miss Frayle, it is useless to ask me for explanations at this juncture. You are fully cognisant of the fact that I do not verbally elucidate my findings until the case is complete.' He walked over to her. 'At the moment we are only at the beginnings of our investigation. It behoves us now to proceed cautiously to discover the murderer, bearing in mind that he is, of course, a dangerous person and may be armed.'

'Oh dear! I don't think I — '

'Kindly do not indulge in negative

speculation.' He added condescendingly: 'No doubt you will prove to be of some slight assistance. You may commence by holding this torch for me.'

He then walked from the workroom into a narrow corridor at the end of which was a door.

'Strange there should be a door here,' he commented. 'Doubtless it leads to the adjoining house.'

He scrutinised the door closely. A hook had been screwed in the woodwork, and over the hook was a piece of grimy string threaded through a cotton-reel and a key. Doctor Morelle grasped the key and inserted it in the lock. It turned easily, as though the lock had been newly oiled. He opened the door. Ahead of them they saw a dimly lit corridor at the end of which were curtains of coloured beads that reflected the brilliant light on the other side.

He walked through the doorway and glanced behind him. 'Observe a hook and key also on this side of the door,' he noted. 'Apparently the deceased and his neighbour had free access to each other's houses.'

'It's all so sinister,' Miss Frayle shivered. Her nose twitched like a rabbit's. 'And this smell of incense. It's quite overpowering.'

'Hm, the unmistakable acid odour of punk sticks as burnt by Orientals — ' He broke off as he heard soft voices from behind the bead curtains. He snapped: 'Follow me, Miss Frayle. It behoves us to investigate.'

He pushed through the clinking bead curtains, and his eyes narrowed as he observed groups of Chinese sitting round low tables playing cards. The Orientals blandly turned to look at him.

'Gentlemen, I fear I am intruding,' he announced calmly.

A tall, distinguished-looking Chinese rose to his feet and shuffled over to him, greeting him with an obsequious *kao-tao*. The Doctor glanced over the man's shoulder at the paper mottoes of green and yellow that were pinned over the pictures. The walls were alight with banners and expressionless masks of scarlet and purple with blank holes where the eyes would be. The other Chinese, he noticed, had imperturbably returned to their gambling.

'I am Chan Lum,' the tall man greeted him smoothly. 'Welcome. You friends of Mister Woodham?'

'I am acquainted with him.'

Chan Lum nodded. 'You and lady come to play fan-tan or puck-a-boo?'

'Thank you — no.'

'Then you partake of refreshment?' the other asked courteously.

'I fear we have no time.' The Doctor lit a Le Sphinx as he summed up the Oriental. Then he said quite bluntly: 'Mr. Woodham has met with an — er — accident. He is dead, Mr. Chan Lum. A suicide note is beside his corpse. I am Doctor Morelle.'

Chan Lum's impassive features immediately registered distress. A low moaning sound escaped his lips.

'*Ay-eiou.* Him my good friend. So sad.' He lowered his almond eyes. 'He would not do this. We good friends. My house is his and his mine. Observe the keys on the doors — the keys of good friendship.' He moved near to the Doctor. 'This news makes me sad — so sad.'

Doctor Morelle glanced across to the card tables. 'Did he ever participate in games of chance with you?'

'Yes. He liked game.'

'Did he suffer much financial loss?'

'No. He often win. I would not let him lose. He my friend.'

'Do you know if he had any enemies?'

'No. Everyone love him. He so kind. He hear nothing evil. He say nothing evil. He understood — everything — *Aye-eiou*.' Chan Lupi moaned again.

'Did the deceased ever receive any visitors?'

'Many — yes.'

'His nephew? Did he come here?'

'His nephew — Bert French? Yes.'

'What did Woodham do in his recreation time?'

'He play puck-a-boo here. Sometimes he go for refreshment to the *Commercial*, *Charley Brown's*, the *Blue Post* — not often.'

Doctor Morelle moved to the bead curtains. 'Thank you,' he nodded briefly. 'You will remain here, I take it, should I

213

require to question you again?'

'I stay here,' Chan Lum murmured silkily. 'I light joss stick for my poor friend. Sad — so sad.' He shuffled across the room, moaning softly.

Miss Frayle followed the Doctor, who opened the door to Woodham's shop and closed it after him.

'Poor man,' she said sympathetically. 'He seemed so upset,' She straightened her shoulders. 'I didn't feel a bit frightened. He was such a nice man. I think he really was terribly grieved.'

The Doctor clicked his tongue enigmatically as he strode through into the shop and made his way behind the counter.

'Kindly train the torch in this direction, Miss Frayle,' he ordered briskly, 'and take care your carelessness does not precipitate any of the demised's timepieces to the floor.'

He was inspecting some ledgers, and quietly voiced his elucidations: 'Woodham regularly banked his profits, so could not have lost much to his Chinese companions. Hm . . . considerable cash balance, but no entry that he has banked this week. Strange.' He inspected a heavy drawer that was let into the counter. 'This would be the till, Ah! Scratches on the brass lock, indicating it had been picked.' He pulled the drawer open. The smooth slanting surface was empty. 'Devoid of moneys. Quite obviously robbery was the motive.'

'How terribly callous to kill and rob a deaf-mute for his hard-earned money!' Miss Frayle burst out. 'I think it's awful and — ' She pointed urgently to the floor. 'Look, Doctor — a glove near your feet.'

'Unusually observant of you, Miss Frayle,' he conceded. He bent down, picked up the glove and examined it. 'Odd that anyone would wear gloves in the middle of the summer. Precaution against digital impressions, I presume. New glove — evidently purchased for the occasion.'

'It's the left-hand glove,' Miss Frayle exclaimed excitedly.

'Thank you.' His tone was quietly sarcastic. 'Apparently the perpetrator of the homicide and robbery found he could not manipulate the lock while hampered

215

by a glove. He therefore removed the glove and carelessly mislaid it!' He gazed at Miss Frayle penetratingly and rapped out: 'What does that indicate about the homicide?'

'Well, that he was — er — well, careless?'

'Brilliant. Quite brilliant, my dear Miss Frayle! Anything else?'

'Well — er — no.'

'Does it not make it apparent even to the most cretinous intelligence that the homicide is patently *left-handed*?'

'Oh, of course.'

'At last we have a basis for further investigation.' He half closed the till-drawer. 'Would it be quite futile, Miss Frayle, to ask for your suggestion as to what we should do next?'

She straightened her spectacles. 'I know! We can go back to Chan Lum's, watch the men playing cards, and see if any of them deal left-handedly. Then we have the murderer.'

He bowed mockingly in acknowledgment. 'I am pleased to observe you are not completely devoid of resourcefulness,' he remarked. 'However, I do not think — '

He stopped short, his fingers gripping the edge of the till. Through the beam of the torch a huge figure, which had entered through the doorway, was moving to the counter.

Abruptly a sepulchral voice boomed through the darkness.

'You'll be having plenty of time to think, mister. Plenty!'

'Oh — save me, Doctor!' Miss Frayle had already taken cover under the counter.

'Good evening, officer,' Doctor Morelle was saying calmly. 'I did not apprehend your approach.'

'So it seems,' the policeman nodded suspiciously. 'The shop door being ajar invited me to look in, and just as well, too by what's been going on.'

Miss Frayle's head appeared over the counter. 'You — you don't think we have had anything to do with this?' she stammered.

'Maybe you have — maybe you haven't,' the policeman declared in hollow tones. 'That's what I'm going to find out.'

'I am Doctor Morelle, officer. This

tremulous species of femininity is my assistant, Miss Frayle.'

'Maybe you are a doctor.' The policeman smoothed his chin thoughtfully. 'And then again, maybe you ain't.'

'If you doubt my credentials, you have only to telephone Detective-Inspector Hood at Scotland Yard.' Then he snapped quickly: 'May I ask *your* name?'

The other was taken aback. 'Oh well, Toombs is me name,' he grunted.

Miss Frayle breathed: 'It would be.'

'Spelt with two O's,' the policeman went on.

'And is it your usual custom,' the Doctor interrogated briskly, 'to wear the top buttons of your tunic unfastened in such a slovenly manner while on duty?'

'Wot's it ter do with you, I'd like to know?' the policeman muttered darkly, and pointedly refrained from fastening up his tunic. He gave the Doctor a sharp look, and then seemed to thaw slightly although it was quite apparent that he was still suspicious, 'Stay here while I have a look round,' he grunted. 'And no monkey tricks.'

218

A minute later Police-constable Toombs reappeared with the slate on which was written the death message. 'Huh, you'd think after being deaf and dumb all these years — born like it he was — '

'So I understand,' murmured the Doctor.

'You'd think old Woodham would've carried on till his proper time came.'

Doctor Morelle eyed the massive policeman condescendingly.

'The taking of his own life may have been governed by a number of factors not wholly concerned with his incapacity,' he pronounced. 'One might speculate at length, but without complete cognisance of the essential fundamentals of his psychological background, the answer might not be forthcoming.'

'Er — quite,' the other grunted, completely in a mental fog. He moved to the door. 'Now you just stay here with the body, Doctor — and the lady too,' he instructed, 'while I go to the station and make a report to the Inspector.'

'Kindly proceed with all expediency,' the Doctor said, as the policeman lumbered into the street.

'Well, I never!' gasped Miss Frayle, 'I think at first he thought *we* had something to do with it!' She blinked up at the Doctor. 'Why did you tell him all that rigmarole to make him think poor Mr. Woodham had committed suicide?'

'If I had informed him as to the true facts, his presence would have been prolonged, and as was only too obvious from his manner, he would have obstructed our investigations.'

She fiddled with her spectacles. 'I've a theory he was not a policeman at all! He was just dressed up as one — stole or borrowed the uniform — and he came back here for the incriminating glove!'

Doctor Morelle laughed sardonically. 'It would indeed have been fortuitous if he had been able to procure a uniform to fit his outsize dimensions.' He tapped a Le Sphinx on the counter. 'I fear you are indulging in fantasia, Miss Frayle, encouraged, no doubt, by too frequent visits to the cinema. However, you have voiced one particle of reasoning. It is logical that the perpetrator of the crime might return for the glove which he so carelessly mislaid.'

'So we just stay here and wait for the murderer to come back and attack us!' Miss Frayle quavered. 'I wish I'd never come with you. I wish I was still in bed. I wish — '

'If you are afraid of being attacked, then it might be more judicious if you would extinguish the torch, which makes you, I fear, a somewhat conspicuous target.'

She clicked the torch off quickly, although the alternative was to crouch there in the eerie darkness. They waited almost half an hour, Doctor Morelle noting the time on his luminous watch dial. His brow deepened in a frown as he pondered why the police officer was such a long time returning. For one second, he actually wondered whether Miss Frayle's theory that the unusually disrespectful policeman was indeed an impostor, had any rational foundation, but he quickly discarded the thought. Since the hypothesis had emanated from Miss Frayle's illogical reasoning then, by the law of averages, it must be inaccurate. Not that he wished the appearance of the police at this stage. On the contrary the longer they kept away the more chance there would be of the murderer's returning.

His conjectures were interrupted as he heard a steady creaking from the door. A shaft of moonlight shone through the aperture, and a smallish, dark-clad figure appeared. Doctor Morelle held Miss Frayle's arm — not in solicitude, but to discourage her from screaming. The figure in the doorway paused. Then there was the scratching of a match, and a pale face was revealed in the yellow light. The man, who was youngish, walked to a gas jet and lit it shakily. Deliberately the Doctor coughed and walked round the counter.

The youth turned quickly, his features twitching. Despite his heavily-padded shoulders and his widely cut trousers, he was a very weedy-looking specimen indeed.

'Wot the blazes you doing 'ere?' he demanded nervously. 'Standing there in the dark, giving a bloke a turn!'

'I might ask you the same question,'

Doctor Morelle said levelly.

'Oh, you might, might you?' the youth flashed. 'Well I've a right to be 'ere. Ain't Mr. Woodham my uncle? Can't a bloke look in to find out how his pore old uncle is, when he sees his door open?'

'But of course,' the Doctor agreed in a strangely mollifying tone. 'You'll be Mr. French, I gather.'

'That's me.'

'I am Doctor Morelle, and this is my assistant, Miss Frayle. We are here too on your uncle's behalf. Your uncle and I have been acquainted for a considerable period.'

The other lost some of his nervousness when he noticed the Doctor's apparently friendly manner, though his beady eyes still moved shiftily. 'I s'pose Uncle's in bed and he's left you to close up the shop. He hasn't been took queer, has he?'

'Your uncle, I fear, is unwell.'

'Sorry to hear that.' The young man fingered his lips nervously as though he were craving a cigarette.

The Doctor, taking his cue quickly, withdrew his gold cigarette case from his pocket, snapped it open and held it out.

'Take one.'

Miss Frayle drew back to the wall as she watched the youth's hands come forward, first his left then his right. She clapped her fingers to her mouth to stifle a scream as, without any clumsiness he took the cigarette with his left hand.

Imperturbably the Doctor walked towards him, and held his lighter to the cigarette tip. The other inhaled deeply, then took the cigarette between the thumb and fore-finger of his left hand.

'Thanks,' he grunted. 'I was parched for a smoke.'

'It appears you are left-handed?' queried the Doctor smoothly.

'Eh?' — self-consciously transferring the cigarette to his right hand.

'And you are not naturally ambidex-trous as you would now have us believe.'

'I dunno wot you're talking abaht.'

'Do you not?' Impassively Doctor Morelle withdrew the left-hand glove from his pocket. The other started, screwed up his eyes in the smoke and snapped the brim of his light fawn trilby with shaking fingers.

'This, I believe, is yours?'

'No it ain't — I dunno anything abaht it — I — ' Flustered, eyes darting from the tell-tale glove to the Doctor's saturnine features, he backed towards the door. He saw the suspicion in Doctor Morelle's eyes, and the horror-stricken look on Miss Frayle's face. 'I tell you — it's a mistake. I dunno — '

Lights danced on his pointed patent leather shoes as he spun round, dashed through the door, and flung it closed in Doctor Morelle's face. The Doctor wrenched it open and strode into the street, followed by Miss Frayle. Moon-light illuminated Cleft Street. There was no sign of their quarry. He had disappeared. Either he was in hiding in a shadowed doorway, or had darted into another house. Or he might have escaped down a narrow alleyway at the corner of Chan Lum's house.

Grasping his swordstick Doctor Morelle moved down Cleft Street with swift strides.

'Don't leave me, Doctor. Wait for me!' Miss Frayle called.

They paused as they reached a causeway that branched off Cleft Street. From out of the shadows a massive black form appeared, blocked their path and, with an angry growl, pounced on the Doctor.

Doctor Morelle sidestepped, but could not escape the grasping hands that reached from the darkness.

'Ho, no you don't,' a hollow voice boomed. 'Thought you'd get away, eh? Pretending to be a Doctor, were you? Well, I thought I'd watch you — and now you're coming to the station.'

'Release me this instant!'

'Not blooming likely.'

'You're making a terrible mistake, officer,' Miss Frayle protested. 'Oh, Doctor — what — ?'

She gasped in amazement, as she saw him grasp the huge policeman by the wrist and elbow, jerk quickly and throw him headlong to the pavement.

'Come on!' he snapped. 'There is no time for apologies.'

The policeman sat up half stunned, and cursing volubly. He blew a shrill and prolonged blast on his whistle.

With Miss Frayle floundering after him, the Doctor sped down the street. Ahead of them, at the river end of Cleft Street, the wharves, with cranes and derricks were silhouetted gauntly against the skyline. Miss Frayle grasped the Doctor's arm tightly as she caught sight of a dark figure running up the gangplank of an old tramp steamer.

'There he is — going aboard that ship! Look, Doctor!' she cried wildly.

'Yes, yes — so I perceive!'

Skilfully making his way round ropes, packing cases and cables, Doctor Morelle paced across the wharf towards the gangplank.

The young man was darting over the deck of the tramp, trying vainly to discover a hiding place. Now they saw him kneeling and tugging at a battened hatch. He glanced round him, disappeared behind a funnel, and was next seen half crouched, wriggling his way aft. As Doctor Morelle ran up the gangplank, he drew himself upright.

'Go back,' he screamed madly. 'I'll let

you have it. I'm warning you — '

Relentlessly the Doctor proceeded up the gangplank.

'Look out, Doctor,' shouted Miss Frayle, 'he's armed!'

Moonlight glinted on a revolver in his hand as he backed across the deck, eyes blazing like those of a cornered animal.

'I'm going to shoot — '

There was a spurt of flame and a report.

The Doctor fell heavily, grasping Miss Frayle's waist and pulling her down with him. They lay motionless — Miss Frayle paralysed by fear and the Doctor — ?

'Doctor! Are you all right?' she gasped, frenzied with anxiety.

There was an agonising silence before he said:

'Yes, Miss Frayle.'

'Are you sure?'

'I am sure I am not quite dead,' he said with a sardonic chuckle. 'Judging by your vocal volume, your injuries are no more serious than abrasions caused by your timely fall — '

She raised her head. The Doctor jerked

it down. More bullets flew over them in quick succession. She trembled uncontrollably, convulsed with panic, her throat burning and her heart beating like a jungle drum. It seemed an eternity as bullets pinged round them. One, two, three — five! For fifteen seconds she ceased to breathe. Then she heard the repeated clicks of an empty revolver, and slowly she became conscious that she was alive, and that the Doctor's arm was round her protectively.

'Fortuitously our friend would appear to be a singularly inferior marksman,' he was commenting, as he helped her to her feet. He advanced slowly. French was backing to the edge of the deck.

He stood there, feet planted apart, trapped but desperate, the tension of his figure indicating he was ready to fight it out to the last.

As the Doctor approached, the other grasped his revolver by the barrel and lifted his arm high, ready to strike with the heavy butt.

'You won't take me — you won't,' he screamed.

'Drop that weapon and put your arms up,' the Doctor commanded, still walking forward across the deck.

'I won't, I'll — I'll kill you too.' His lips curled malevolently as he saw the Doctor halt. 'Ah, I thought that would stop you — no, no!'

His voice became a yell as he saw the Doctor twisting the top of his swordstick to reveal its steel blade.

'Throw down that gun — this is your last chance!' Doctor Morelle ordered, moving forward with the sharp blade-point thrust forward.

The other spun round, turning his back on them. His thin figure grew taut. He shot out his arms, glanced downwards fearfully, and dived into the river.

'He'll drown! Oh, what shall we do?' gasped Miss Frayle, running to the edge and peering over.

Already Doctor Morelle was stripping off his jacket.

'You can't go after him!' she tugged at his arm. 'You might drown — catch pneumonia. He isn't worth saving.'

Doctor Morelle stepped to the edge,

preparatory to jumping over. She still clung to him.

'Release me, Miss Frayle, this instant.'

'It isn't necessary, Doctor. Maybe he can swim — ' she cried wildly.

The wash lapped against the wharf, as they peered below to where a fawn trilby floated down the river. Then a dark head appeared and an ashen white face showed above the murky water. The arms of the youth threshed, and with steady strokes he began to swim away from the docks.

'He can swim. Thank heavens!' Miss Frayle breathed fervently. Her eyes were brimming as she touched the Doctor's arm. 'I think I'd have died with worry if you'd gone in after him.'

Doctor Morelle put on his jacket again. His piercing gaze followed the flashing arms as the man swam towards midstream.

'It may be still necessary,' he murmured. 'He cannot possibly swim to the other side.'

'He's making for that tug — fifteen yards out.'

'So it would appear.'

Tensely they watched the progress of the swimmer. Both breathed freely again as they saw him reach the tug, grasp a rope and exhaustedly crawl aboard.

'I am constrained to believe,' observed the Doctor as he contentedly lit a Le Sphinx, 'that the young man will be only too relieved when he is arrested by the river patrol. He must be singularly damp.'

He turned round and strode across the wharf. A group of men lumbered up in the moonlight. Miss Frayle discerned three in police uniform, among them the unmistakably mammoth form of Police-Constable Toombs.

'I'm Inspector Dent,' one of the men introduced himself. 'You'll be Doctor Morelle. Thank heavens you're safe. We heard shots and — '

'Quite so, Inspector,' nodded the Doctor, calmly flicking the ash of his cigarette. 'The man you want has conveniently marooned himself on that vessel over there!'

Toombs moved towards Doctor Morelle sheepishly.

'I've got to apologise,' he said in a

hollow voice. 'Sorry I was suspicious. All in line with my duty. Hope you're all right — '

'Perfectly,' the Doctor nodded curtly, and added philosophically: 'Over-conscientiousness is, fortunately, a rare virtue.'

Then he stared piercingly at the policeman's bulging tunic. Flushing hotly, Toombs hurriedly fastened the recalcitrant buttons.

★   ★   ★

Later — and inevitably — Miss Frayle was questioning Doctor Morelle in his study, concerning his brilliant elucidation of the case.

'Of course,' she observed, 'if you hadn't been so clever as to realise it wasn't suicide, you wouldn't have known it was murder. And if you hadn't known it was murder, you wouldn't have bothered to track down the murderer.'

He smiled thinly. 'Your capacity for cool, logical reasoning positively astounds me, my dear Miss Frayle,' he said with faintly derisible sarcasm.

She smiled sweetly, ignoring his gibe. 'I'm just dying to know how you knew it was murder and not suicide — I mean — even before you discovered Woodham had been robbed, you knew he had not killed himself.'

'That was so. The fact was, indeed, made crystal clear to me in the note purported to have been written by Woodham, but which was actually forged by the murderer. Had Woodham himself written it he could not have mis-spelt the words 'nephew', 'yours', and 'despair' by writing them down phonetically. A deaf-mute from birth, he would never have heard words pronounced and could only have learned to know them by sight, correctly spelt. The consequent elucidation was complete and unfailingly accurate — '

'But there's one mysterious point you have failed to elucidate, Doctor,' she pointed out, with an impish smile.

He raised his eyebrows quizzically. 'And what is that, Miss Frayle?'

'Who made the anonymous telephone call telling us of the clockmaker's death?'

He clicked his tongue impatiently.

'We are not in the least concerned with his identity,' he retorted briskly. 'To know the name of the mysterious caller does not in the least affect the outcome of the case. It is quite irrelevant.'

'You mean you don't know — and can't find out!' she taunted annoyingly.

'I do not wish to find out!' he snapped hastily. 'Really, Miss Frayle, your preoccupation with trifles and inconsequent details is symptomatic of the feminine attitude to — '

Mercifully for Miss Frayle, he was interrupted by the ringing of the telephone bell.

'Perhaps that's the anonymous caller now!' she said with a gay laugh.

'I cannot imagine anything so coincidental,' barked the Doctor, 'but if instead of smirking at the telephone you would perhaps be good enough to answer it, we might ascertain the identity of the caller.'

'All the same, supposing it is the mysterious — '

'Kindly do as I ask!'

She lifted the receiver. 'This is Doctor Morelle's house. Who is that, please? Oh

— oh, I see. Would you hold on?'

'What is it, Miss Frayle?' he demanded through tightly clenched teeth.

'It isn't the man, anyway, Doctor,' she evaded irritatingly, 'it's a lady, and she's in great distress, she's — '

'Come to the point. What does she want?'

Miss Frayle smirked and paused deliberately before she answered: 'She wishes to know if you'd help her trace her pet canary — '

'What — !'

'Which flew off this evening, and hasn't come back, and answers to the name of Terence . . .'

THE END

LEATHERFACE
DR. MORELLE MEETS MURDER
A CASE FOR DR. MORELLE
DR. MORELLE'S CASEBOOK
DR. MORELLE INVESTIGATES
DR. MORELLE INTERVENES

We do hope that you have enjoyed reading this large print book.

Did you know that all of our titles are available for purchase?

We publish a wide range of high quality large print books including:
Romances, Mysteries, Classics
General Fiction
Non Fiction and Westerns

Special interest titles available in large print are:
The Little Oxford Dictionary
Music Book, Song Book
Hymn Book, Service Book

Also available from us courtesy of Oxford University Press:
Young Readers' Dictionary
(large print edition)
Young Readers' Thesaurus
(large print edition)

For further information or a free brochure, please contact us at:
Ulverscroft Large Print Books Ltd.,
The Green, Bradgate Road, Anstey,
Leicester, LE7 7FU, England.
Tel: (00 44) **0116 236 4325**
Fax: (00 44) **0116 234 0205**

ROSES FOR A LADY

John Glasby

Edith Somerville, great-granddaughter of a wealthy banker in L.A., received two-dozen red roses with a note attached: she would receive one rose less every day and on receipt of the last rose she would die . . . Private Detective Johnny Merak sets out to find the would-be killer and when certain members of the family are murdered, Johnny finds proof of yet another, earlier, murder. But it's not until Edith receives the final rose that the killer is unmasked . . .

RETURN TO AKADA

John Russell Fearn

Rich widow Rita Perrivale returns to the coast of West Africa on a new expedition to the legendary lost city of Akada and its treasures. She only survived the first, disastrous expedition due to the help of Anjani, a white man, raised in the jungle by a native tribe. But Rita, hoping to be reunited with Anjani, hasn't reckoned with the treacherous Tocoto, Anjani's twin brother — and his rival for the supremacy of the Dark Continent . . .

DR. MORELLE INTERVENES

Ernest Dudley

Doctor Morelle and Miss Frayle await the last train to London . . . at its approach, the village station attendant rushes to open the level crossing gates. Later, however, on the train, they learn that following a fatal crash, the station's level crossing had been replaced by a bridge! Exactly five years earlier the stationmaster had been killed as he vainly attempted to open the gates. And on the anniversary of the disaster, it's reputed that his ghost returns . . .